THE RETIRED S RANKED ADVENTURER 5

Wolfe Locke, James Falcon

COPYRIGHT

Copyright © [2023] by [Wolfe Locke]
All rights reserved.
No portion of this book may be reproduced in any form without written permission from the publisher or author, except as permitted by U.S. copyright law.

CHAPTER 1: WELCOME HOME

Tom Riley, once known as Sven the Shatterfist, a legendary adventurer in a world left behind, now stood as the owner and head chef of The Rustic Grill. His sleeves rolled up to his elbows revealed heavily muscled and scarred arms, reminders of battles fought and won, as he expertly flipped a burger on the grill. The heat made his skin slick with sweat, but he didn't mind. He pushed it away with the back of his arm and wiped his forehead with a towel.

As the burgers sizzled on the grill, Tom's vision blurred as he reached for the basket of freshly cut potatoes, the world around him seeming to glitch momentarily. A semi-transparent overlay sputtered into existence, flickering and unstable like an old TV trying to find its signal. It was filled with a scattering of distorted images that battled to form coherent shapes. Slowly, they resolved themselves into shaky, flickering letters, which read, 'Cooking Skill Level: 71.' The message strained against the static, before it corroded.

It was a relic, a ghostly echo from his past life, a faded memory of a world where every action held a measurable value. It was a quantifiable skill from a time when he had stood as the strongest man and had surpassed the values those old system screens used to represent.

He wasn't sure it was even real and kept it to himself. He ignored it and kept up his work. Tom reached for a basket of freshly cut potatoes and lowered them into a pot of bubbling oil, watching as they turned a golden brown. The scent of frying potatoes mixed with the aroma of grilling meat, made his mouth water.

The restaurant was bustling with customers, each table filled with people laughing and chatting over plates of delicious food. Tom could hear the clinking of glasses and the murmur of happy conversation, a sound that never failed to make him feel content. It was a testament to the hard work he and his wife, Ash, had put into it over the years ever since they'd crossed over through the rift.

As the burger sizzled on the grill and the fries fried in the oil, Tom reached for a freshly baked bun and spread a generous amount of the "family" secret sauce on it. The sauce was a mixture of tangy cranberry jelly and smoky barbecue sauce. He and Ash always claimed it was a recipe passed down through generations of his family. Usually when questions were asked about his family and where he was from, Ash would utter something about Europe. She now defaulted to saying he was from somewhere European and vaguely Finnish.

It was a lie, albeit a small one. In this world, Tom's family was Ash and Kaleigh, he didn't have anyone else and hadn't for a long time. The recipe had been Ma Riley's, at least as close to hers as he could remember. He then added a few slices of ripe tomatoes and a handful of lettuce, carefully arranging them on the bun.

Tom fished the fries out of the oil, shaking off the excess and transferring them to a wire rack. He sprinkled them with another pinch of salt before grabbing a handful and popping them into his mouth when he thought nobody was looking. They were just right. Crisp and salty, a perfect complement to the juicy burgers he was working on.

Once the burger was nearly cooked to perfection, Tom placed a slice cheese over the burger, watching as it slowly melted from the heat. Still gooey, he slid it onto the bun and added a few slices of dill chips on top to finish it off.

He admired his handiwork for a moment before carefully transferring the burger to a plate and adding a side of crispy fries newly emerged from the fryer, adding seasoning salt as another layer of flavor.

As he seasoned the fries, danger senses put him on edge, but just for a moment. It was a sensation he hadn't felt in years. The same sensation he used to feel before a battle. He shook off the feeling, attributing it to a past that occasionally bothered him, *especially* in his dreams.

He glanced over at Ash, who was busy mixing drinks at the bar. Her hair was a vibrant shade of red, and her eyes, once red, had turned a deep shade of blue. The blue suited her, although her red were once reminders of her days as a powerful mage in another world. One that they had left behind for some years now.

To Tom, her blue eyes represented their new lives, what they had built with their own hands here in her world. Those red eyes were her past, left behind along with her magic, legacy, and trappings of the system of the world. Tom loved these eyes. They were softer, more subdued, but more importantly—they sparkled with joy. He'd had years now to watch her blue eyes. To see the wisdom filter through her eyes when she spoke to those around her, the light when she stared at him and their daughter. His wife had been by his side through a lot of upheavals.

Tom grinned, thinking of how lucky he was and grateful for everything they had built together.

Their daughter, Kaleigh, darted between tables, taking orders and delivering food with a bright smile on her face. She had inherited Tom's brown hair, and unfortunately his strong, square jaw, but there was just enough hint of Ash's clumsiness to remind Tom of just who her mother was. She had a boundless energy that never seemed to flag, even as the dinner rush hit its peak. Tom rang the bell when it was ready for Kaleigh to grab and serve.

"Order up!" He called out with a grin.

Kaleigh smiled. "Thanks dad. I got it."

Tom felt a sense of pride wash over him as he watched his family work together, the restaurant alive with energy. This was his life now, the life he had worked hard for, and he wouldn't have it any other way. Tom turned back to the kitchen, grabbing the next ticket and went to work. The order was for a well-done steak. He grimaced, knowing that cooking a steak beyond medium was basically a crime. But it wasn't his order, and he had a business to run.

A business that someday he wanted to pass on. Hopefully to his daughter.

Tom chuckled heartily. It was true. Kaleigh would soon be graduating, stepping into a world far safer than his own had been at her age. Yet, he couldn't help but wonder. *What would her future look like?* She was born into a world he'd merely adapted to, her challenges wouldn't be his. Fatherhood weighed on him.

As he turned back to the grill, a sudden feeling of unease washed over him. It started as a small knot in his stomach, but quickly spread throughout his entire body. Tom paused, his hand hovering over the grill as he tried to pinpoint the source of his discomfort.

The unease quickly turned to pain, a sharp, stabbing sensation in his chest. He clutched at his chest, trying to catch his breath, but the pain only intensified. Almost instinctively, a transparent notification popped up in his blurry vision.

Tom stumbled backwards, his vision blurring as the world around him seemed to twist and warp. He heard Ash calling his name, but her voice sounded muffled and distant. His heart raced as he felt himself being pulled apart; his very essence stretched thin. He reached out for Ash, trying to hold her hand, but she seemed to be fading away. His hand passed through the notification that hung in the air.

"Hold on, Tom, hold on!" Ash's voice was loud in the chaos of the Grill. Each word soaked in years of love, memories, and shared battles across worlds. It wasn't just a wife calling for her husband, it was a partner who had stood at his side, their fates intertwined, screaming out to the universe for the man she'd defied destiny to be with.

The man she could not bear to lose.

"Kaleigh call 911!" She managed to scream out, struggling to form the words. Her hands shook as she fumbled for the phone, but her eyes never left him. "You're going to be ok. You have to be ok!".

Each word was a plea, a desperate prayer flung to whatever god or gods might be listening. She had seen him fight monsters, seen him stand victorious on alien worlds, and now she was seeing him brought to his knees by an enemy he couldn't fight, and neither could she.

Age.

"No, Tom, please," Ash sobbed, hot tears welling up and spilling over her cheeks. She begged, her voice barely a whisper as people in the restaurant moved tables and made way for the emergency services. "Stay with me, Tom. Don't you dare leave me, not again.

Another system alert flashed before his fading vision.

With an effort that took everything he had left, Tom tried to push himself up off the floor. His intention was to reassure her, to stand up and show her he was alright. The memory of her pleading voice, that desperate edge he had never heard before, propelled him to fight against the pain threatening to drag him under.

"Ash..." he managed to croak, though his voice was barely recognizable to his own ears. He could feel the cold sweat on his brow, the trembling in his hands.

He gave a strangled grunt as he tried to hoist himself up, the room spinning around him. He could make out Ash's form in his blurring vision, a flurry of movement as she reached for his hand even with the numbness creeping through his body.

"I'm... okay..." he stuttered, even as his knees buckled beneath him. It was a feeble attempt, and they both knew it. His strength gave out, and he collapsed back onto the floor, his body no longer able to support him.

His words were garbled, incoherent, a far cry from the confident assurance he intended. His world tilted dangerously, his vision narrowing until all he could see was a blur of color and light.

"Hang on, Tom," she whispered, her voice a lifeline he was finding increasingly hard to hold on to.

"DAD! DAD! HELP IS COMING!" Kaleigh screamed as she rushed over. Her voice was practically breaking. Time passed and he faded in and out of consciousness. The sounds of his two favorite people were blending into background noise.

The front door was thrust open, letting in a

burst of evening air and the sounds of sirens in the distance. The thump of heavy boots against the hardwood floors, the authoritative commands, the rustle of equipment being unpacked. Noises filled the restaurant.

"EMS, on site!" a voice announced, taking control of the panic. Faintly, Tom could just barely make out the blurry figures of paramedics.

Firm hands hoisted him from the floor, sliding onto the firmer surface of a gurney they set beneath him. A groan slipped past his lips as a new wave of pain rolled over him, originating from his chest and radiating outwards in cruel tendrils.

The pain in his chest got worse. Tom felt as though he were being pulled apart, his very essence stretched thin.

His heart beat faster, thudding against his chest and they moved, shouting commands at each other. His breathing was labored. Voices yelled at him, but he couldn't focus. The room spun and moved. The sound of ambulance sirens and bright lights followed, only to be replaced by a blinding light that completely covered him.

The world shifted, with Tom at its center. It morphed in a dizzying spectacle that defied any sense of reality he had known. The familiar sounds of sirens and concerned voices faded into a dissonant echo, replaced by an intense, all-encompassing silence. His very surroundings dissolved and corroded into pixels. Almost like the system message he got earlier. His mind tried to cling to the smell of grilled food, the ambulance, brewing coffee, and even to the noise of people shouting... The silence bled it all away into nothingness.

He plunged into an infinite abyss. There was no time here, nothing but emptiness. He couldn't even feel his body. Just a barely coherent mind sucked into the dark. Then—like the stories Kaleigh had enjoyed reading about—a tunnel of shimmering, vibrant light stretched out in front of him, leading him away from everything he knew. Then he blinked in surprise, there was sensation. He could *feel* again. Although he couldn't see his body, nor move it, the fact he could feel was puzzling and exciting. The first sensation he felt was... falling. It was odd though, this felt like he was at the top of a steep hill in a car before going down immediately on the other side.

Then... unfamiliar sensations followed. It wasn't heat or cold, nor was it tactile. It was gossamer—like passing through layers, silky strands on your skin to know you'd passed something, but left unsure what it was. Yet, a niggling memory was triggered by this sensation... if only his mind could focus for longer than a second he would understand why this sensation was familiar. He noticed scents next. The smell of ancient stone, damp earth, and musty air...

As his eyes adjusted, he could make out the cold stone floor beneath him and the dim, flickering light that illuminated his new surroundings. His mind tried to grapple with the transition, attempting to reconcile the impossible shift.

"Ash! Kaleigh!" Tom's voice echoed throughout the stone chamber, the names of his wife and daughter reverberating off the ancient walls. But there was no response. The crypt was silent save for his own voice and the quiet drip of water somewhere in the distance.

He was alone.

A sense of wariness ran down his back as he slowly got to his feet, his heart pounding in his chest. He looked around the crypt, desperate to find some sign of his family, some indication they were there with him. But there was nothing. Only the cold, damp stone and the fading glow of a summoning circle, similarly used to the world he had once known.

His mind raced, struggling to piece together the events of the last few moments. One minute he was in his restaurant, feeling the sharp, agonizing pain in his chest—the next he was here, in this unknown place... in the center of a summoning circle no less. He recalled Ash's terrified face, Kaleigh's tear-streaked cheeks, the frantic rush of the EMS team... The many notifications from the time he got the level up skill for cooking and right up to now. They must have been warnings, a precursor. But he didn't want to believe it. He couldn't.

A few realizations hit him with cold, numbing shock. "I died... or I was summoned as I died." he whispered to himself. As soft as they were, the words echoed in the silent chamber. It was the only explanation that made sense. He had died in his restaurant and somehow, he'd ended up here, in a new world.

But where did that leave Ash and Kaleigh?

A new wave of fear washed over him, a bigger panic then he'd felt when he'd been struggling for breath on the restaurant floor. *If he was here and they were still there, what would happen to them?*

"I have to get back to them," he said to himself, his voice resolute. He didn't know how he was going to do it, but he knew he had to try.

CHAPTER 2: WORLD REBORN

The notification faded gradually. Tom sat down trying to puzzle through the wave of confusion and uncertainty that only seemed to magnify with each unanswered question in his mind. His eyes, having adjusted to the sparse light, revealed a world locked in a timeless vacuum. It was a cavernous expanse, veiled by the gloom of the forgotten past. The air was heavy with the scent of old stone and the echoing solitude of centuries.

The walls were adorned with intricate etchings, each wall told a story, spread out like panels depicting a man in battle against various beasts. His eyes widened. *He knew these battles*. The sight of these elaborate designs brought forth a cascade of memories from the corners of his consciousness. *This was like a trip down memory lane.* Images of him adorned the walls from his days as an adventurer, when he had battled monstrous creatures, overcoming dungeons, and defeating the monsters who controlled each dungeon as a boss. *He'd lost friends too.* His past life completely adorned the space, leaving him nostalgic... oddly, there was a pull to this place now that he had time to calm down. Almost like the place was welcoming him home.

"Where am I?" He muttered.

He rubbed his eyes, "That works." The flickering torchlight cast long shadows across the ancient stone, the ghostly flames an unearthly blue that spread across his face.

In the midst of the shadows, something caught his attention. His heart thudded in his chest as his gaze found a towering silhouette looming over him. Squinting through the darkness, the statue came into focus, revealing a figure strikingly familiar—a figure that was his own... just younger. Chiseled into an imposing pose, arms crossed, the stone figure embodied the persona he was remembered as—Sven, the Legendary Adventurer. The visage held a stern, determined expression, but in the eyes, Tom saw a glimmer of warmth—an eerily accurate portrayal of the man he used to be.

It was a conundrum.

Yet, despite the unfamiliar surroundings, Tom was comforted by the area. He knew dungeons. He knew how they worked. And this crypt was not so different from the many he had conquered in the past.

It sparked something within him. He may have been taken from his grill, from his family, but he had been returned to a world he understood.

Half-forgotten memories came unbidden to his mind. *The challenge, the monsters, the fighting. All of it. The satisfaction of a cleared dungeon*—these were sensations he had tucked away as his past, like an attic full of antiquities. And now, they were his hope, an anchor in a world that was familiar… but changed.

"It's just another dungeon," Tom muttered. "I used to stroll through places like this."

With a newfound determination, he rose back to his feet and hardened his resolve. This was a crypt, a dungeon to be conquered. *He would find his way out and return to Ash and Kaleigh.*

After all, he used to be an S-Ranked

Adventurer. It was time to remind this world of that fact… right after he practiced his rusty skills on the dungeon monsters likely roaming down here.

"I need to channel the adventurer I once was," Tom mused, mentally flexing a skill set that had been dormant for years. "This place… it's still a dungeon. Dungeon's have rules. And if it is a dungeon, it won't be empty. There will be monsters. Crypt-dwelling monsters. Undead."

Focusing his thoughts, he centered, taking deep breaths and stilled. It was an adventurer's mindset, an old muscle, but one ingrained deeply within him. The world may have changed around him, but dungeons were still dungeons. With a smile he found himself stepping back into an all too familiar role. An adventurer… *Just like the old days.*

"Undead," he echoed, the word carrying a weight of its own. His eyes swept the shadowed crypt once again.

Skeletons and ghouls were a given, but experience taught him to expect more. A slight smile tugged at the corners of his mouth as one particular type sprang to mind - Wraiths. He remembered destroying the roof of the bosses' room and carrying Ash out.

It had been a good memory.

The shelves around him bristled with mystical tomes and objects radiating an uncanny dark glow. His gaze swept over these curios, in search of something, anything that could be of use.

"The first rule of being an adventurer—always have a weapon," Tom muttered to himself, attempting to move, only to find his body rebelling against his commands. Exhaustion threatened to sink its claws in, but then, an unexpected shift occurred.

The summoning circle beneath his feet flared one finale time and then abruptly vanished. It left behind luminous motes of aura that danced around him like an ethereal serpent. As it encircled him, a revitalizing energy pulsed through his veins, stirring within him dormant power.

He straightened up, the dim torchlight flickering in the distance only enhanced the haunting quality of his surroundings. Cobwebs clung to the corners, and layers of untouched dust spoke volumes about the dungeon's disuse. Whoever, or whatever, had drawn him here had long forsaken this place.

There was an unexpected tinge to the

sensation, a faint undertow pulling at his senses. He could almost hear a faint whisper in the back of his mind, a murmuring akin to a spell being woven around him like an insistent reminder at the back of your mind. It wasn't overpowering, merely distracting and inconvenient.

With the summoning circle gone, the room felt, empty. That sense of belonging had faded with the spell and Tom felt the urge to move onwards.

"Find a way out and make it back home to my family." he mumbled and strode off into the flickering gloom of the room.

Harsh sounds of battle erupted in the distance echoing off the stone walls. The grating clash of steel, enraged roars, and desperate yells.

And that is why an adventurer needs a weapon. Tom looked around and on a rotted looking table his gaze landed on an ancient sword, its rusted blade peeking out from beneath layers of dust and grime. It was unimpressive but far better than being unarmed.

"Been awhile, but should do in the meantime," he told himself, picking up the sword. Its worn grip seemed to mold into his hand, an almost perfect fit. Even with time, his hands hadn't lost their callouses and his grip. Time in the kitchen had kept up that edge.

A guttural growl boomed through the corridors, followed by the emergence of a monstrous figure from the shadows. Its glowing eyes locked onto Tom. Its monstrous form—that of a giant lizard, donned in mismatched leather and chainmail armor, wielded a menacing saber.

Tom eyed the monstrous figure, a smirk playing at the corners of his mouth. The bizarre circumstances might have beaten down any other man, but Tom—he was built of sterner stuff. "You're not the undead I was expecting," he said, the faint traces of amusement lacing his tone. The creature snarled, probably not understanding his words but catching his defiant spirit.

"Bit more scale than I anticipated," Tom added, his grip tightening on the hilt of the ancient sword.

With an agile lunge that would have been impossible for Tom just an hour before, he attacked. The Ancient Blade hissed through the air, striking against the creature's scaled hide with a satisfying thud. He couldn't suppress a chuckle, "You know, I've dealt with worse. I've been to Florida."

Unfazed, the Lizardman retaliated, snarling as it brandished its saber with surprising agility. But Tom was ready, his blade meeting the creatures in a clash of steel. He sidestepped, taking advantage of the beast's momentum to deliver a swift cut to its side. The Lizardman hissed in pain, its yellow eyes flashing menacingly in the dim light.

Tom fell into a fighting stance instinctively as the creature lunged. The rhythm of combat, of attack and defend. Lunge and parry, flooded back to him. His footwork was precise, his body recalling the art of kata patterns from a time when overwhelming power hadn't been his go to.

The lizardman's attack was parried easily, his movements echoing an elegance and agility he hadn't felt in years. *He was back in the game. The fight was on.*

"Wow, touchy," Tom remarked, grinning as he started to feel more at ease, more himself.

The Lizardman lunged, his movements growing more desperate. Tom's ancient blade met the creature's strike, a burst of sparks lighting the dim crypt.

"Watch it, you'll dull my new blade," he chided, sidestepping another frantic swipe and retaliating with a swift jab that sent the creature reeling backward.

As the Lizardman stumbled, Tom seized the moment. His movements were quick, and he easily evaded the creature's desperate strikes. The Ancient Blade cutting into the Lizardman.

Tom smiled.

There was something about the fight, something about being alive that reminded him of his days as Sven, the Shatterfist. A part of him he'd all but forgotten.

The grin that split his face was wide. "Ah, Ash, you'd have loved to see this," he mused, wishing she could witness him coming alive in this way.

The Lizardman, however, wasn't done just yet. With a last-ditch effort, it swung its tail like a whip, trying to catch him off guard. Tom saw it coming. The world seemed to slow down as he leapt; his body silhouetted against the flickering torchlight.

I still got it.

With a perfect arc, he vaulted over the creature's tail, using the momentum to drive the rusty blade deep into its side. The blade sank in with a sickening squelch, the sound of victory echoing in the dungeon.

"End of the line, pal," he said.

The Lizardman let out one last hiss, its breath rattling in its chest as its body slumped to the cold stone floor. The creature's life force, a swirling red energy, rose from its body, dissipating into the darkness of the dungeon.

CHAPTER 3: AWAKENING

Panting heavily after his brief skirmish with the Lizardman in the dungeon crypt, Tom yanked the Ancient Blade free from the rapidly vanishing corpse of the monster. When the blade came loose, Tom found himself staring at his reflection on the edge of the now-pristine blade. The rust that had once marred the Ancient Sword had come away, leaving a sharpened edge underneath. The blade had more to it than initially thought.

Sven looked down and recoiled at the sight of what he found reflected on the steel surface. A younger face peered back at him. A *much* younger face. The once prominent wrinkles of age and burden of years were erased, replaced completely by the youthful visage he remembered from his prime when he had been Sven the Shatterfist.

"Would you still recognize me, Ash?" He wondered.

The question would have to wait, as would the how of getting home.

Swirling orbs of light caught the corner of his eye, generated from where the lizardman had perished. They blended with the lingering red aura of the slain creature and magnetically drifted towards him, spiraling around his body in an ethereal dance. He could only watch as the orbs of light circulated and phased through him.

A voice echoed within his mind, its tone clear and commanding. It was an encompassing presence, one he hadn't felt for a long time. Like a dormant system that was now springing to life, it pulled, adjusted and activated pathways within him that hadn't been in motion for years.

That's new. Tom's eyes narrowed, wondering what was happening. The orbs of light were seemingly initializing some type of process that he was completely unused to.

Alright, so back to the old ground, but at the beginning. Things could be worse. The system had reset, and he was back to square one, now with the raw stats of an F-ranked novice. The values were close to what a muscular and athletic 25-year-old would be, a *far cry* from the legendary adventurer he had once been.

As Tom grappled with the revelation, another screen popped up.

Tom held his breath, hopeful of regaining some of the formidable abilities of his former glory as Sven the Shatterfist, a man more or less without equal who bore the blade Worldrender and had been capable of superhuman feats.

"Just give me something good," He muttered.

Alright, I guess that's better than nothing, but what am I getting? Tom waited anxiously to see what the System would designate for him.

"This is nice, not quite what I'm used to, but it's nice enough" Tom yelled out, "But how exactly does this get me home?

Taking a deep breath, he acknowledged the name that had once completely defined him.

Sven, then. It's time to be Sven again. Over the years, he had yearned for his former life as Sven, wishing his daughter Kaleigh could have met that version of him—the hero, the adventurer, rather than a simple cook.

"Sven it is," he reaffirmed.

He evaluated his surroundings, deciding his first action would be to follow the lizardman's trail, hoping it would lead him towards some answers.

As the System finalized his status and the orbs of light finally dissipated, leaving him alone in the crypt once more, Tom thought of the reflection he had seen in the steel of his blade. That younger face—Sven the Shatterfist, the warrior who once stood against armies, who held aloft Worldrender and commanded respect and fear in equal measure.

That was the man he used to be. That was the man he wanted his daughter to know. The man who had been a hero.

Swallowing the lump in his throat, he traced the edge of his weapon with his fingers. Kaleigh had only known him as a humble cook who made her laugh with tales, she never believed in a world that felt too extraordinary to be true. She had never seen him swing a sword, had never witnessed the power with which he used to move, nor seen him kill a monster or achieve anything more superhuman than feeding hungry customers during a rush hour.

Sven the Shatterfist to her was just another bedtime story she'd grown out of.

He had kept that part of his life hidden, not out of shame, but out of an intense desire to protect her from things she wouldn't understand. There was no way to tell a child, even one that was grown up as she was, that he'd come from another world.

If anything, she'd have thought him a liar or crazy, and when he and Ash had come to Earth, he had thought it was a one-way journey. But now, in this world that was so much like his old one, he realized that he wanted to share that part of him with her. Not to show off or to boost his ego, but to let her know who he truly was, beyond the quiet man who tended the grill at the restaurant.

"I wish you could see me now, Kaleigh," he murmured. "I wish you could see the man your father once was. I will always remember when I was Sven the Shatterfist."

CHAPTER 4: SPIDRENS

"All right, not sure when this happened but I'll go with it," Tom, no *Sven* murmured, giving a firm pat to the worn armor he was wearing as he stepped further into the shadowy tunnel. His voice echoed back at him. The name 'Tom' no longer applied in this world.

He was Sven. He had to be Sven.

"New challenge. What do I know?" he asked, purely for his benefit to gather his thoughts.

This self-talk was an old habit, forged in the crucible of his early days as an adventurer in the Near Islands. The strategy was simple: break down the impossible tasks into manageable chunks, analyze it, strategize, and act.

It was one of the methods that had helped him

survive during that first year when he'd been a ship's cabin boy journeying from the Kingdom of White Lions. The routine had become unnecessary as he matured, his hard-earned wisdom, battle prowess, and instincts taking their place.

But today, he found himself falling back into old patterns.

"I'm twenty-five again," he said, his voice echoing off the damp stone walls. A dry chuckle slipped past his lips. "And—gods help me—an F-ranker."

His age had regressed, his warrior's physique and stamina returned, a stark contrast to his graying hair and softened muscles back on Earth. Even though his youth had returned to him, his strength hadn't, and he was currently equipped with the skills of a new adventurer.

"But just because I'm a F-Ranker now, doesn't change who I was, or what I know how to do." He paused. Was he enjoying this?

The battle, the adventure, the excitement. It all came rushing back, igniting a fire he'd thought long extinguished. He loved his peaceful life with Ash and Kaleigh—the satisfaction of grilling burgers, the smiles as he served a plate of fries—but there was more to him than that, and the part that had been Sven.

The thought made him shake his head.

"Yeah Tom. Eyes on the prize." He scolded himself. His mission was to return to Earth, to his family. Everything else was secondary.

"Back to the question. What do I know?" The man took in everything. "Alright, I'm in the world for a reason. I have to be. Someone, or something has brought me here. If I find the source that brought me here, I'll understand more of why I was brought and then…"

"Home." He muttered. "The long way home. Nothing else matters."

The man ran his fingers along the stone wall, the damp stone grounded him and his thoughts. The dungeon crypt was an underground system of tunneling halls, chambers, and rooms. His escape and answers would likely lead upwards.

Upwards it is.

The planning was interrupted by a high-pitched laugh echoing down the tunnel. His senses were immediately on alert.

"A trap? Possibly." He muttered. But it could also be his only lead, and as he had once learned, it was only a trap if he didn't know it was before him. He clenched his jaw and carrying the Ancient blade kept moving towards the sound, not away from it.

Subtle scratching noises against the stone followed. An old sound that prickled at the edge of his senses as memories struggled to place just where he had heard the sound before.

"Ah... hell... its spiders."

He looked around and from behind him was nothing but the empty chamber he'd left behind. While ahead a nightmare of skittering legs and red eyes approached.

"Sometimes, in the absence of fire, the only way out is through." He gripped the Ancient Blade tight and prepared to cut a path ahead.

Without a moment's hesitation, the first of the spiders launched themselves at him, a frenzied wave of monstrous bodies and jagged fangs. These creatures, the size of small dogs, their eight beady eyes gleaming with malicious intent, were familiar. Sven had slain many during his adventures and many variations.

Even if he wasn't as powerful as he had been. He wouldn't lose to spiders.

Drawing a deep breath to steady himself, he got into a fighting stance. He would need to count on his experience. Not magic, not special abilities.

Not overwhelming strength. He had only the basics, but they'd have to be enough. He would find a way to enhance his strength later.

Sven's grip was firm as his hands completely enveloped the hilt of the Ancient Blade. He readied himself as the approaching spiders lunged, their venomous jaws dripping and eager. Truthfully, *so was he*. His eyes, sharp and calculating, remained locked onto the monstrous creatures. Well-honed reflexes poised for the impending battle. As they swarmed into range, Sven executed an effortless swing of his blade, a lethal slash of steel cutting through spider chitin with ease.

Mere spiders couldn't impede his journey in this dungeon.

With a swift, practiced motion, Sven sprang into action, his well-worn blade followed a deadly trajectory through the damp, chill air of the narrow crypt corridor. It found its mark in the hulking form of the nearest spider. Recoiling in surprise, the creature erupted into an enraged jarring chittering sound, clicking its mandibles while trying to attack in a frenzied display of anger and pain.

"Well, that got your attention, didn't it?" Sven murmured, a grin touching his lips. His tone was light, but his eyes remained cool and calculating.

Ignoring the creature's furious response, Sven pressed forward, propelling himself into the heart of the fray. He maneuvered around the spider's desperate attacks with expert skill, nimbly evading venomous fangs with a speed and agility born not just from his younger body, but the practiced experience of a lifetime. With a sweeping stroke of controlled power, he targeted the spider's soft underbelly. It emitted a high-pitched scream before collapsing onto the cold, stone floor.

Yet, the battle was not over. The dying screams of the spider echoed menacingly through the passage, rallying the remaining spiders towards Sven. Their fallen spider's death knell sending them into a frenzy, rushing towards Sven.

"That's not good enough," He laughed.

He met their charge head-on. His movements, a whirlwind of steel and motion. The Ancient Blade met each attack with deft parries and lethal strikes, finding its mark with deadly precision time after time.

"But you lot are persistent, aren't you?" He chuckled, never missing a beat,

However, the battle was far from over. The

death of the spiders was not silent. It was a call that summoned the remaining spiders towards Sven. They rushed him. Sven's resolve hardened, and he met them head-on.

"Just had to work out the rust. That's all." He laughed looking ahead at the coming spiders.

His movements were a blur, his blade whistling through the air as the rhythm of battle surged through him, rekindling old memories of countless battles within dungeons. His blade expertly parrying and striking, finding its mark with deadly accuracy with every attack.

Despite how easily Sven dispatched the spiders, the monsters were undeterred. They came and came again. They seemed to multiply with each passing second, their endless numbers threatening to overrun the narrow passage.

En mass, the spiders writhed in a chaotic sea of legs and fangs in their attempts to be the first to overcome him. Sven hardly noticed. Even when his arms started to grow heavy and sluggish with the weight of relentless combat.

For someone like him, victory was all but assured.

He had a goal. He was nothing, if not persistent. He had a family waiting for him—Ash and Kaleigh. They were his beacon, his guiding motivation in the face of this monstrous horde. Digging deep to ignore his aching muscles, he pressed onward. Though the creatures may have had the advantage in numbers, they lacked the cohesion of a tactical mind. They weren't thinking creatures, merely reactionary. Besides, he had something they didn't.

Experience.

Using his combat wisdom, Sven studied the spiders, observed their tactics, their patterns. He anticipated their moves, and countered with lightning-fast agility, leaping and rolling out of harm's way. Each time they lunged and missed, he capitalized, retaliating with swift and deadly strikes. The spiders started falling, one by one, their monstrous bodies crumbling and disappearing under the careful strikes of the Ancient Blade.

It took longer than he expected to finish them all off.

When it was done, Sven looked at the Ancient Blade and shook his head.

"Can't wait until I get a real weapon."

CHAPTER 5: UNDEAD

Sven pressed on through the crypt dungeon, skirting the sticky remnants of the defeated spiders. The dungeon's absorption of the fallen creatures had already begun, leaving traces of ichor that stuck unpleasantly to his boots.

"Ash. Kaleigh. They're counting on me." That was his mantra as he kept going.

As Sven navigated the crypt, memories of his past adventures with Ash resurfaced. Her spellcasting skills had often been the decisive factor in their battles, her playful banter and steady support was just as effective as a well-placed spell.

The void left by her absence gnawed at him. He couldn't help but wonder if she'd missed these days of adventuring just as much as he had. It wasn't something they'd talked about much. They had a silent pact to let it lay in the past, neither had ever thought they would be able to return. Oddly enough, this was a conversation that neither of them had ever initiated. It was as if they were mutually apprehensive to voice these thoughts, fearful that their humble existence in the diner could never truly measure up to the thrill of their previous lives.

Footsteps echoed from down the hall, interrupting him from his musing with the steady patter of approaching. The crypt's air turned rank, heavy with the scent of decay. Dancing shadows signaled the arrival of an undead legion on the ancient stone. An uncanny blend of skeletal warriors and reanimated corpses staggered towards him, their movements somehow blending an awkward clumsiness with a horrifyingly graceful malevolence. Their hollow eye sockets bore into him, exuding an aura of relentless hunger.

"Figures, this is what I'd been expecting," He shrugged.

With a yell, Sven brandished the Ancient Sword bracing himself for the imminent attack.

His battle earlier against the spiders had already awakened his combat instincts. This battle was even easier for him. Predicting their actions, his blade cut through decaying flesh and brittle bones, reducing his adversaries to dust.

Despite being outnumbered, Sven was never in any real danger. He pressed on, letting the familiar rhythm of combat—parry, thrust, strike—overcome him. The crypt became an echo of steel clashing against steel and cutting into bone.

The undead fell to his sword.

In the thick of the melee, Sven noticed a strange pattern—his opponents exhibited an unusual level of coordination, atypical of their kind. A gut instinct warned him of a greater danger lurking within the crypt, a feeling amplified by the familiar yet chilling laughter echoing closer. Although he was aware of the crypt's deceptive acoustics, he still felt annoyed.

"Just another obstacle to clear to get home,"

One notion crystallized in Sven's mind amid the tumultuous chaos of battle: there had to be a commander. The uncommon organization and coordination amongst the undead were signs of a leading force.

Even as a seasoned S-Ranked adventurer,

Sven knew better than to dismiss the undead lightly, particularly in a crypt dungeon where the prevailing air of death empowered them. Still, he was well versed in combat strategy: eliminate the leader to scatter the horde. This approach had served him well in the past, and so he pressed onward, each defeated undead marking his progress through the crypt.

It didn't take long for the floor of the crypt to be briefly littered with remnants of fallen enemies before being reabsorbed back into the dungeon. Sven moved with a fury, needing only simple attacks and none of the F ranked abilities the system had bestowed on him.

The undead were many. They clamored and tried to reach for him, even as his sword swept through their ranks in unstoppable wide arcs.

As Sven delved deeper into the crypt, the undead manifested in more of their variations. From the gaunt skeletons clanking with rotting clubs to the fallen warriors, their rusty swords and axes still clutched in decaying grips.

Yet, Sven remained almost single mindedly focused as he destroyed the undead. Using the narrow confines to his advantage, he pushed off the cold, stone walls, propelling himself through the oncoming undead with agility and purpose.

His blade was a blur. He cut down the approaching undead with a grim resolve, his strikes precise and fatal. Each swing of his sword shattered skulls, every attack aimed to destroy. The crumbling bones sounded like brittle twigs before disappearing back into the dungeon.

The undead tried to counter, but not one was able to land a blow on him. He weaved between their attacks, his deft movements disrupting their coordination and providing him with openings to counterattack. He crushed the skull of one and shattered the spine of another, never once did he stop.

Despite the persistent battle, Sven was far from weary. His earlier fatigue had changed to a battle furor the further he fought, another trait that made him so impressive and dangerous as an S-Ranker. He moved through the crypt's corridors with ease. His mission was far from over; there was still the Lich or greater undead that controlled the rest of them.

His experiences had taught him that in order to eliminate the leader, he'd find it further among its minions. They used their minions as fodder to weaken and tire out their enemies, preferring overwhelming force. However, these minions were more regimented; had a variety of undead in groups like an adventurer party set up. In his experiences that meant he was looking for a Lich. Hence why, he needed to be quick and decisive and smash his way through rather than be methodical and destroy one at a time. Lich's would just respawn their minions given enough time. Destroying the Lich, in particular, would throw the horde into disarray, rendering them significantly less of a threat. Yet, Sven noted that the enemies weren't respawning... *perhaps he was killing them too fast for the Lich to keep up?* Either way, he needed to go faster.

And so, as Sven battled his way through the mass of undead, the crypt floor transformed into a grotesque mosaic of strewn bones and decaying flesh. His eyes darted across the battlefield, scanning for a Lich. The enemies came and Sven destroyed them.

"There you are!" Sven smiled.

A towering skeletal figure loomed above the rest. Its skull was adorned with a weathered bronze helmet, its mouth open in a mute, ceaseless scream. Though speechless, the pointed finger it aimed at Sven sufficed for communication.

Answering this silent command, a fresh wave of undead advanced, their lifeless gaze locked on him. Determined to end this, Sven carved a path through the crowd, pushing towards the Lich. As he neared his target, the air grew icier, and the odious scent of decay intensified.

"Gods," Sven grimaced, "I despise the undead." The memory of the countless undead he'd dispatched at the kingdom of White Lions was etched deeply into his memory. It was a long drawn out affair with constantly respawning enemies. The cold, clinging odor of decay was a constant reminder of the foes he faced. The Lich, undoubtedly, would be a challenge unlike any undead within the dungeon so far, but it was still only a Lich, he'd fought against plenty and come out ahead.

He kept moving. Sven tightened his grip around the hilt of his sword, bracing himself for the impending battle. He dashed forward, the dank crypt air whipping past him as he charged toward the Lich. With a fearsome roar, he lunged, aiming his weapon at the skeletal creature.

But the Lich was faster. With a mere flick of its hand, it summoned a magical barrier that deflected Sven's attack. The force of the spell propelled him backwards, and he stumbled, nearly losing his footing. The stone floor was damp and cold beneath his feet, slick with a film of ancient crypt slime that threatened to betray his footing at the most inopportune moments.

Shaking off the surprise, he focused his attention back on the Lich. He could see the creature muttering an incantation under its breath, its skeletal fingers tracing cryptic symbols in the air. A sharp chill ran down his spine; he recognized that spell.

"Sven, dodge!" he shouted at himself, his instincts screaming at him to move. He sprang to the side as a surge of dark energy was unleashed from the Lich's outstretched hand, crashing into the spot he had just vacated. The crypt shook with the impact, the ancient stone walls shaking under the force of the spell.

Using the shockwave as a boost, he pushed off from a protruding stone, closing the distance between him and the Lich. The ancient crypt's tight space worked to his advantage. He spun, cutting through the air and aimed at the Lich's skeletal frame. He struck true; his sword slashed through the creature's tattered robes, cutting through layers of bone.

The Lich shrieked; its voice made up of a handful of souls. In a last-ditch effort, it swung its metallic staff in retaliation. Sven barely had time to raise his sword for a block; the weapons clashed with a loud ring.

A battle of wills ensued, steel meeting steel in a dangerous dance. Each strike sent shockwaves through the crypt. Sparks flew and ricocheted off the walls, casting sporadic, dancing shadows on the grimy stone floor.

Sven pressed his attack. He knew he couldn't let up; the moment he did, would be the moment he lost. His muscles screamed in protest, but he pushed past the pain. His sword was an extension of his will, matching the Lich's staff strike for strike.

In the end, it was a reckless swing from the Lich that provided Sven his opening. He dodged the wide arc, stepped into the creature's defenses, and drove his sword into the center of its skeletal frame. The Lich's form exploded in a cloud of dust, its piercing shriek echoing throughout the crypt.

For a brief moment, Sven stood there, panting, his sword still held aloft. The crypt fell silent except for the sound of his heavy breathing.

"No. That couldn't have been a real Lich.

Maybe just a Skeletal Mage." Sven muttered under his breath, disappointment etched on his face. He couldn't help but feel let down. He had been so sure he was dealing with a Lich. *The tactics were similar*.

His next words carried a self-deprecating laugh. "A Lich is at least A-ranked. What was I thinking?" Sven scolded himself, a wry smile pulling at the corners of his mouth. His time in the quiet life had evidently dulled his monster-assessment skills.

Things changed.

The undead that had been surging around him stilled in the aftermath of the Overseer's defeat. The connection between the minions and their leader had been severed, leaving them aimless. The monsters going into a state of dormancy once more. Their rotting limbs sagged, their aggressive postures relaxed, and their hollow, hungry eyes dulled and then returned to the system.

It was nothing Sven wasn't familiar with.

CHAPTER 6: CAVE TROLL

Once the Skeletal overlord was defeated, mopping up the rest of the dead was easy work. They lacked the simple cohesion they had before and mulled about in the crypt tunnels aimlessly without purpose, barely even registering Sven's presence until he was already on them.

Even as underpowered as he was in his F-Ranked state, someone like Sven could hardly be inconvenienced by lesser dead. He moved forward through the passageways, slashing, striking, and bashing as he went.

Soon he was alone once more in the tunnels with only the rapidly disintegrating remnants of enemies behind him as they returned to the dungeon.

Mocking laughter soon followed. He smiled thinking on the first time he'd heard ominous laughter in his first dungeon. He'd been so green. Nervous, nearly jumping at every sound the dungeon made.

Now, he merely sighed. The sound seemed to be closer than it had been previously. Sven gripped the Ancient Blade and kept moving, knowing sooner or later he'd be face to face with that voice. Eventually, the dungeon crypt expanded and the stone ground gave way to dirt and the loose rocks of a larger cavern.

"Of course, there would be a cave," Sven muttered as he looked around. There were flickering torches mounted on the walls and large stalactites hung from the ceiling, dripping with cold water and a massive chasm that separated one side of the cave from the other. From what Sven could tell it was the only way forward, and on the other side of the chasm was a monstrous cave troll.

When it saw him, it let out a massive roar and raised its massive club.

"It's not too late!" Sven shouted, "If you look the other way and let me pass, I'm willing to just let you be."

The cave troll kept coming.

Sven shrugged. "Worth a shot."

He set his feet in a fighter's stance as the troll lumbered toward him. The monster was slow but undeniably powerful. Each step the troll made, the ground shook and rocks fell to the cavern floor. When it got closer, the monster's massive club, as gnarled and as colossal as the troll itself—swept through the air with enough force to kill a man.

Sven dodged. His movements quick and agile compared to the troll's sluggishness. He darted in seeing a weakness and nicked the trolls arm with the Ancient Blade. The monster swung the club again in a counterattack that was much quicker than the previous. Sven ducked under the blow and could feel the rush of air above his head as the club whistled past him.

Adrenaline fueled his body. Pushing him towards the usual weak point of trolls. A joint.

He lunged forward, trying to strike at the troll's lower body. His sword clashed against the thick, stony hide around its ankles; the blow sent shockwaves through his arm. It was like hitting granite and the sound was loudly echoed in the cavern. The troll grunted, unaffected, and kicked out with a foot larger than Sven's entire body.

Sven was sent flying backwards, crashing into a stalagmite. Pain exploded in his shoulder, but he gritted his teeth and pushed it aside.

"No time for pain, that's just weakness leaving the body," He grunted.

He staggered back to his feet, shaking off the blow. His breath came in ragged gasps, the stench of the troll now mixed with his own sweat.

He watched as the troll turned and raised its club for another strike. Sven eyed the troll's movement, his mind racing. In the midst of the pain, he remained calm. Like all monsters, there had to be a weakness, he just had to find it. Then he saw it, a small patch of lighter gray on the troll's lower back.

"You've fought somebody else before. A wound that didn't heal right. That'll do." Sven grinned, feeling satisfied.

With a surge of determination, he sprang forward, dodging a sweeping strike from the troll's club. He felt a rush of air as he sprinted toward the troll. It was a risky move, a bold one, but it was one of the best of options.

He stabbed d at the troll's weak spot. His sword bit into flesh, and the troll roared in pain.

"Success!" He laughed and moved before the

troll could hit him with another counter.

The cavern was filled with the sound of the troll's rage. The fight wasn't over, but Sven had found an opening, and with an opening, he would win.

A grin was replaced by steely resolve as he prepared for his next attack. His body ached, and his breath was labored, more from the damage he'd taken than from exertion. This was what he lived for, what he'd missed most, the thrill of battle, the test of skill, the chance to prove his worth. And he was far from finished.

He stabbed again.

The monster pivoted and lashed out. In a swift motion, the troll swept its massive arm around, attempting to swat Sven away like an annoying insect. Anticipating the move, Sven rolled to the side, the rough cavern floor scraping against his armor. The troll's vicious backhand barely missed him.

Pushing off the ground, Sven sprung up and darted around the beast. The troll, despite its earlier brutishness, was clearly disoriented, its movements slower and more desperate. It seemed the wound on its back was more debilitating than Sven initially thought, a piece of luck he thanked the old gods for. The echoing, guttural moans of the troll filled the cavern, amplifying the sense of imminent victory.

But Sven was a seasoned fighter. He knew better than to be complacent and that an injured monster was even more dangerous.

With his every muscle tense and ready, Sven continued to circle the troll, now favoring agility over force. He focused on wearing the troll down, landing rapid, stinging strikes on the same weakened spot.

Each strike was a battle in itself, a test of Sven's dwindling stamina against the troll's immense strength. Sweat stung his eyes, his arms felt heavy as lead, but he willed himself to keep moving. His heart pounded in his chest like a war drum and propelled him forward.

The troll raged and swung its club overhead in a last desperate attempt to crush Sven. But Sven had seen it coming. With a battle-hardened will, he lunged forward and slid underneath the troll's legs, narrowly escaping the club's destructive descent. The ground shook as the club slammed into the spot Sven stood just a moment ago, throwing up chunks of the cavern floor.

Sven pushed himself off the ground and

attacked again. His sword found its mark again and stabbed into troll's back, driving deeper this time. The beast let out a bellow and staggered forward, dropping to one knee. A sign that the tide of battle had turned.

Victory was close, he could taste it. Sven drew in a ragged breath, raising his sword high, and with a yell that rivaled the roar of the troll, he brought the sword across a vulnerable spot on the trolls neck. The sound of steel slicing through flesh and bone followed by the thud of the troll's severed head hitting the floor. The cavern fell silent except for the harsh panting of the victorious warrior.

Every inch of Sven's body felt tired after the fight, but he couldn't help the grin that spread across his face.

"I did it. I won." He goofily grinned and felt his legs almost buckle like they were jelly. He stumbled over to a stalagmite, sliding down its base to sit. He leaned his head back trying to catch his breath while his stamina recovered.

As he looked over at the rapidly disintegrating body of the troll, Sven couldn't help but feel a kinship to the monster, a sense of belonging. This place felt *right*. It was only a troll, but it represented familiarity. He snorted, there was a time when a troll would have been nothing for him, but for now, it was a start, and he'd managed it.

He was alive.

Sven reached for a flask underneath his armor. He'd found it glinting near one of the crypts while traversing the dungeon.

"To you, ugly," he toasted, "You were a worthy opponent, and you reminded me of who I am, of why I do this. Here's to you, and to the thrill of battle!" He tipped the flask back, grimacing as the fiery liquid seared its path down his throat.

He savored the heat that spread from his stomach, igniting his veins with a warm glow. It felt good. More than good, it felt right. He was in his element, living the life he was meant to.

Sven could almost forget the ache in his limbs, the sweat drying on his skin, the exhaustion gnawing at his bones. For a moment, he allowed himself to bask in the victory, to appreciate the return of the feeling he had missed so much— the feeling of being alive, of being in a fight, and winning it.

"I'm back," he murmured to the silent cavern, an uncontainable grin stretching across his face, "I'm truly back.

CHAPTER 7: ONE STEP FORWARD

Sven's moment of triumph was interrupted by the sound of familiar, high-pitched laughter. It was sinister and the dungeon positioned it to make it sound uncomfortably close—almost like it was reverberating from just ahead.

"I hear ya," he mumbled, a small smirk curling the corner of his mouth. Yet, the chilling echo had enough power that it pricked his skin with unease. *A debuff skill or spell... interesting.*

Pushing himself up from his brief reprieve, he navigated around the swiftly decaying remnants of the troll. He entered a passageway on the far side of the cavern, his weapon held ready as he cautiously proceeded.

"Hilarious, isn't it?" he muttered to himself with a sarcastic edge. "Spiders, shambling undead, even a cave troll, all under one roof."

This assortment was unusual. Such a range of monsters weren't typically encountered by any new adventurer starting their journey—let alone, conveniently bundled into a single dungeon. It wasn't just peculiar; it was virtually impossible to occur naturally.

"Nah, this is no coincidence," Sven surmised, his voice bouncing off the cool stone walls. "This is someone's doing. And I bet it's our cackling friend's idea of a joke."

His annoyance grew, manifesting as a low growl under his breath. However, his irritability was somewhat overshadowed by the creeping fatigue. Years of relative inactivity, combined with his current F-Ranked status, were taking their toll. He'd taken on three significant battles in rapid succession, and the exhaustion was beginning to set in. Rest was what he needed, but there was no telling what was waiting for him ahead.

With renewed caution, he advanced along the passageway, noting the slight upward slope under his worn boots. A small smile formed on his lips.

Going up was a good sign; it typically meant he was closer to reaching the surface.

Turning yet another bend in the tunnel, he stepped into a vast cavern. It was a mirror image of the previous one, including the flickering torches adorning the walls and casting dancing shadows on the stalactites overhead. But this one was not occupied by a solitary, gigantic troll.

Instead, a congregation of figures awaited him, their faces concealed by the hoods of their dark robes. They were clustered on the opposite end of the cavern, their bodies still and alert, like statues carved from shadow. The moment Sven emerged, they collectively shifted, looking towards him with an eagerness that was almost tangible.

"Well, this just got interesting," Sven muttered to himself, clenching his hand tighter around the hilt of the Ancient Blade. His heart pounded in his chest as he stared down the mysterious figures. He was weary, yes, but the adrenaline of yet another challenge sparked a familiar fire in his veins. He was far from finished; his adventure was only just beginning.

A feeling of strange familiarity washed over Sven as he eyed the hooded figures. This, somehow, felt like the place he was meant to end up.

"Demetrius," a soft voice called out, directed at one of the robed figures. The voice, urgent yet hushed, repeated the name again, jarring the individual named Demetrius out of his apparent daze.

With a sudden "Oh!", the short figure looked up, quickly catching sight of Sven. "Could it be him?" the first man asked Demetrius, his voice filled with anticipation.

"By the grace of the gods," Demetrius responded, raising his clasped hands toward the ceiling, his face filled with awe. "It very well might be."

A scowl formed on Sven's face. He didn't appreciate the mysterious chatter about him, and the hidden faces did nothing to assuage his growing irritation.

"Hey!" he bellowed, lifting his weapon aloft, its gleaming blade reflecting the dim torchlight. "Who exactly are you lot?"

"I'm not convinced it's him," interjected another figure, skepticism lacing his voice. "He doesn't quite match the painting."

"Of course he doesn't! The painting depicts

him as an elder!" Demetrius retorted, his voice shrill with exasperation. "We explicitly wished him to be in his prime when we brought him back, to ensure he could undertake the task. Between the ages of twenty-two and twenty-seven, remember?"

The skeptical figure remained unconvinced, shaking his head in disagreement. "Bone structure remains the same, regardless of age. There should be some resemblance. And honestly—look at him. It's not the same man, you'll see."

Demetrius seemed to deflate slightly, a hint of panic creeping into his voice. "Did we... did we bring back the wrong person? Could we have made such an error?!"

Annoyance flared within Sven. "Enough!" he snapped, the echo of his voice reverberating off the cavern walls. "I'm right here. I can hear every single word!"

Another figure stepped forward, wringing his hands nervously. "Surely there must be a test we can administer? Something to confirm if he truly is the Shatterfist?"

Demetrius turned his attention back to Sven, studying him closely. "He succeeded in the initial trials. He bested the spiders... the troll."

"But those were rudimentary challenges,"

countered the skeptical figure. "A simple warm-up. Any greenhorn with a blade could have managed."

"But he knew of the Undead Mage," Demetrius shot back. "He was aware that destroying the undead requires taking out its leader. That's not knowledge a novice would possess. He is a seasoned warrior."

"I won't deny that," the skeptical figure conceded. "But it doesn't necessarily mean he's the Shatterfist. Many warriors, especially those from the White Lions, would know the same."

Sven's patience had worn thin. His voice echoed through the cavern, drowning out the bickering. "Firstly, if you wish to ascertain my identity, all you had to do was ask. I'm not invisible, I'm standing right here. And yes, I am indeed Sven the Shatterfist, born Tom Riley. And I can only assume you are the ones responsible for this unexpected journey of mine."

The men in dark robes had turned to him, their gazes blank, met by Sven's displeased frown. "Speak now, or I'll demonstrate just what the Shatterfist can do with a decaying blade," he warned.

"Yes," Demetrius quickly conceded, nodding toward his skeptical peer. "I believe a final test is most appropriate."

Before Sven could even blink, the hooded figures congregated into a ritualistic circle and began to chant. He was familiar with most magical tongues known within the Kingdom of White Lions—albeit his understanding was superficial at best; sorcery was never his forte—but the incantations they wove were alien to his ears. In no time, the floor beneath them began to radiate an eerie, pulsating purple light.

"Hold on," Sven protested, his grip tightening around the worn hilt of his weapon. "What are you—"

A thunderous crack filled the cavern. A rift split the floor open, belching thick, obsidian smoke, that swiftly engulfed the room. The chanting men fell silent and retreated against the farthest wall, keeping a safe distance. Sven instinctively understood that whatever was about to emerge from that fracture was not going to be a pleasant surprise. He swiftly relocated himself towards the opposite wall, blade poised and ready, allowing himself the space to respond.

"Alright," he whispered to himself, slipping back into his familiar combat tempo. "Show yourself, creature."

While the hooded figures remained silent spectators, Sven felt their eyes scrutinizing his every move. So be it. They wished to examine his mettle? He would give them a performance they wouldn't forget.

A shrill screech followed the eerie silence as the first reptilian head weaved its way out of the smoke, quickly followed by another, and another, until nine monstrous heads towered above. The beast's body remained veiled by the rift, but Sven needed no further clues. A hydra. Though this was nothing like the hydra he had once so frequently fought.

Even in his prime, this would be a challenging fight, let alone in his current exhausted state. The robed men were practically on the edge of their circle, engrossed as he advanced towards the looming threat, his sword at the ready. Its sinewy hide shimmered under the torchlight, and its myriad heads writhed and snarled, anticipating the imminent clash. Each head sported flaming eyes and venom-dripping fangs that sizzled upon contact with the ground.

An inexperienced, green warrior would have likely dashed forward, weapon flailing in their recklessness. But Sven, bearing the wisdom of countless battles, knew better.

His encounters with hydras were not a rarity; he knew full well the pitfall of rashness. Sever one head, and two more would sprout in its place. Each severed stump would need to be cauterized posthaste to prevent any further regeneration.

Sven gripped the blade tighter. "I'd wager there's more to this than meets the eye."

The strategy to conquer a hydra was no secret, even to fledgling adventurers, and if this was designed to test his aptitude, it was safe to assume that the robed men had an additional, more devious scheme at play. A secondary mechanism to prompt the hydra's regeneration, complicating the battle even further, was not beyond possibility.

"Could it be related to that rift? Only one way to find out." Sven muttered. "At least it's a hydra. I could slay one of these with my eyes closed."

With lightning reflexes, Sven navigated through the hydra's relentless onslaught, adeptly dodging its lethal strikes. He closed the gap between himself and the crack in the cavern floor from which the monstrous beast had emerged. In a calculated yet audacious gambit, he lunged forward, driving his blade deep into the glowing fissure. The floor, still emitting a deep purple glow, began to flicker erratically, and the hooded men pushed forward, curious to scrutinize his actions.

"Demetrius!" a figure from the group yelled. "Demetrius, did he—"

"Silence. Let me see," Demetrius commanded, joining his hands and dipping his head in an attempt to perform a magical inspection. "It seems he's—yes, he's disrupting the regenerative rift field."

"A promising development," another man mumbled. "Indeed, a promising sign."

"Do you believe that I'm the Shatterfist now?!" Sven's voice thundered through the cavern as he plunged his sword deeper into the ground. The hydra screeched in indignation, gnashing its monstrous jaws, yet Sven paid it no heed. If these men needed further proof of his identity, then he would happily oblige.

Even with a fraction of his former strength and an inferior blade, he was more than they had bargained for. He exerted more force, drove his sword deeper, and then the ground ceased to glow. The regenerative enchantment bound to the rift had been nullified.

The hydra roared, its fury palpable as its source of power was severed. But the battle was far from being over. Sven stifled his instinct to taunt the observing men, opting instead to make a beeline for the distant cavern wall where a torch flickered in a metal bracket. Its flame needed to be hot enough for his plans. Behind him, the hydra lumbered out of the rift, its gaze fixed on him.

Despite its swift heads, the beast's body was sluggish and clumsy—a fortunate twist in his favor. Even in his current state, he maintained an edge in speed and agility.

Sven reached the torch well before the hydra's jaws could snap at his heels. Extracting it from its bracket took three attempts and a significant amount of effort—quite the contrast from his former glory when such a task would have been effortless.

But he succeeded and wheeled back to face the monstrous beast, armed with sword and flame. The hydra screeched its defiance as Sven charged, deftly evading its gnashing teeth and decapitating one of its heads with a swift blow.

Seeing the flesh of the severed stump seethe in preparation for regrowth spurred him into action. The hydra's movements had grown faster, more unpredictable in its rage, yet Sven kept the upper hand. He skillfully sidestepped a jaw, rolled under another, and plunged his torch into the beast's wound, halting the regrowth.

The hydra's roar echoed around him as he retreated, torch held aloft to keep the flame alive. He'd need to conserve the flame, lest he struggled to unseat a second torch from its bracket.

As he whirled to face the hydra once more, Sven cursed his current condition. He held his torch and sword aloft, ready for the next round. One of the hydra's heads lunged at him, fast as lightning—but Sven was quicker. His sword slashed and his torch seared, and another head fell lifelessly to the ground.

With a roar of fury, the hydra reeled back, its serpent-like bodies thrashing in disbelief. It had not anticipated such a formidable adversary in Sven, and he seized this advantage, channeling all his might into pinpoint strikes at the base of each remaining head. With each brutal cut, he immediately applied his torch to the wound, searing the flesh before the beast could recover. Each severed head rendered the hydra weaker, its movements increasingly lethargic.

Finally, reduced to a single head, the beast succumbed to pain and blood loss. It slumped to the cavern floor, its convulsions causing the very stone around them to tremble. Sven braced himself, summoning the last of his strength for one final strike.

With a loud crash, the last head tumbled away, severed from its body. An eerie silence descended upon the underground chamber as the lifeless form of the hydra receded back into the rift and disappeared amid the lingering smoke. From the assembly of hooded figures, a slow clap began.

"Bravo, Sven!" Demetrius exclaimed, his voice ripe with genuine admiration. "You've surmounted our ultimate trial."

Sven stood, chest heaving, and limbs weighed down by the fatigue of battle. Yet, he held his gaze steady, even as his posture showed some irritation as he turned to the cloaked spectators.

"Appreciate the compliment," he retorted, his tone laced with irritation. "Now, do you believe I am who I claim to be?"

"To question your identity now would be ludicrous," the earlier skeptic confessed, awe lacing his voice. "The legendary Shatterfist, in our very cavern! I thought such a day would never arrive—"

Sven interrupted him, wiping his sword clean with a ragged piece of cloth. "Save your fanfare for later. First, I demand an explanation for this abduction. I had a life back on Earth, a family I was happy with. Being yanked around like this is not my idea of a good time."

Taken aback, the cloaked men exchanged uneasy glances, their initial excitement quickly wanning under Sven's glare. However, before anyone could attempt a response, the massive iron door at the far end of the cavern swung open with an echoing boom, causing all the hooded men to instantly drop to their knees in reverence.

CHAPTER 8: THE ONE TRUE SVEN

Sven didn't drop to his knees like the others, but he did shift his gaze to the colossal door as it creaked open ominously. The figure about to enter held sway over this peculiar group of hooded men—surely, this leader would be able to provide him with much-needed answers.

"Honor be to the Most Worshipful High Cleric," Demetrius pronounced reverently, his gaze cast down in submission.

"Most Worshipful High Cleric," echoed the chorus of hooded men, their voices carrying a mixture of awe and fear. Sven couldn't help but suppress a groan. He wasn't one for pomp and ceremony, and the ostentatious theatrics of such clandestine societies irritated him to no end.

A raspy voice emanated from the murky shadows of the open door. "Well met, my boys," he croaked, the words echoing through the cavernous chamber. The hooded men parted like the Red Sea, making way for the High Cleric to enter.

He was old, older than anyone Sven had ever laid eyes on. A long, white beard reached almost to the floor, swaying with his peculiar half-shuffle as he made his way into the room. He squinted through clouded eyes, scanning the chamber until his gaze landed on Sven.

"Ah," he croaked, satisfaction clear in his voice. "Our plan was a success. He bested the trial, didn't he, boys?"

"Indeed, he did!" Demetrius responded, his enthusiasm palpable. "Both the preliminary skirmishes and the hydra—"

"Good," the Cleric interrupted, sparing the slain hydra a glance. He shuffled over to its lifeless form, now lying in a puddle of its congealed blood, and sniffed disdainfully. "Guess since it's a rift creature, the dungeon won't take care of it for us."

With a whispered incantation and a series of intricate hand gestures, the High Cleric orchestrated a display of potent magic. The hydra's body slid back into the rift, the smoke swallowing it up, while the gaping hole in the floor sealed itself as if it had never been. He waved his hand and the residual blood disappeared, leaving the stone floor pristine and devoid of any evidence of the fierce battle.

"Much better," the Cleric stated, finally turning his attention back to Sven. "Now, let's examine you more thoroughly."

Sven's eyes flicked over to the High Cleric as he navigated his way across the cavern. The man's skin was papery thin and pale, he felt ancient —unnaturally so—and he emanated an aura of magic so palpable that even Sven, lacking any magical prowess himself, could sense its presence.

I need to watch this one. The old man's got a certain... unsettling vibe to him. Must be S-Ranked. Although I've never heard of him either which is strange...

But it was crucial not to arouse any hostility now; he needed answers. So, Sven remained silent, watching the Cleric's slow approach. Eventually, the old man was standing just a few feet from him, a proximity that made Sven feel somewhat uncomfortable.

"Surprisingly young," the Cleric rasped out, looking Sven up and down. "And conspicuously lacking in power. What of the S-Rank abilities he once boasted?"

"He's currently an F-Ranker—" a hooded figure began, but Sven swiftly raised his hand, silencing him.

"For the third time," he interjected, a harsh edge to his voice as he scanned the gathered men, "cease discussing me as if I am absent. If you've inquiries concerning my identity, direct them to me. I also have a fair share of questions. If it simplifies things, we can take turns asking."

The High Cleric's reaction was impossible to read as he fixed his opaque gaze on Sven. It was almost as if he could sense an undercurrent of magic emanating from the old man's eyes, probing, searching.

Sven narrowed his eyes, *Must be an identify spell. Feel free to probe. I can muster a basic shielding spell.*

Admittedly, he wasn't entirely certain about his abilities. His memory of his F-Ranker skills and the knowledge acquired over the years was hazy. However, when the High Cleric turned away, looking rather irked, Sven knew he'd at least succeeded in preventing the old man from easily extracting the information he sought.

"Fine," the Cleric grumbled. "I concede. You, too, must have questions, lad—"

"Don't call me lad," Sven interjected swiftly.

"Very well. I'll answer your queries to the best of my ability," the Cleric continued, shrugging off Sven's interruption. "Of course, there will be some boundaries. My turn first. Are you truly Sven the Shatterfist?"

"I am," Sven confirmed, his grip tightening on his sword's hilt as a precaution. "However, it's been years since I last used that moniker. Nowadays, I go by my birth name, Tom Riley, and I'm no longer active in the fighting scene. But as you saw, I've still got it. Tell me, could anyone else have vanquished that hydra after years of abstaining from battle?"

The High Cleric dismissed Sven's claim with a wave of his hand. "There are numerous legendary warriors, both real and fictional. Perhaps there are others who could've accomplished the same feat. But I'm inclined to believe you are who you claim to be—the tests substantiated that."

The men, cloaked in their hooded robes, gathered around Sven and the Cleric, maintaining a respectful distance. Sven shifted his attention towards them.

"It's my turn," he declared, looking at each face

in the semi-circle around him. "Who exactly are you lot?"

"We are the Sons of Sven!" Demetrius announced, puffing out his chest with evident pride. "Committed to preserving the legacy of the greatest warrior that ever lived."

Sven blinked in surprise. "I'm sorry, what?"

Demetrius drew himself up to his full height. "We are the Sons of Sven—"

"No, no, I heard you," Sven cut in, slightly exasperated. "I meant, what is this 'Sons of Sven'? Why is there an entire cult dedicated to me? Do all the other warriors have their own fan clubs too?"

He couldn't help but think of his old comrade, Rabbit who was actually a dragon prince who had been cursed and driven from kingdom—he would've reveled in such adulation. But Demetrius was already shaking his head.

"Only you, Shatterfist," he confirmed, his eyes shining with excitement. "As far as we know. It's possible other clandestine groups exist for other heroes, but we're not aware of them. The reality of meeting you...I always believed in your existence, despite the skeptics—"

"I'll confess," interjected the hooded man who had previously expressed his doubts. "I didn't believe you were real. Thought you were more of a metaphor—a symbol of the perfect warrior archetype. Seems I was mistaken! My name's Robin, by the way."

Demetrius chimed in again, his voice filled with awe. "There are so many stories circulating about you. We'll need to confirm with you which are true, and which are mere embellishments—"

The High Cleric sharply addressed his followers, "Silence. We must remember our decorum. We are not a cult, Sven. We are a clerical order, a legacy knighthood, committed to preserving the legacy of the one true Sven."

Sven refrained from pointing out that he couldn't discern much difference between a "legacy knighthood" and a cult. His gut told him that expressing that out loud wouldn't be well received.

"These boys," the Cleric continued, sweeping his hand grandly towards the crowd of hooded figures, "were orphans when I found them. I became their guardian, their mentor. I taught them the art of magic and the skill of combat—when my strength permitted me to. I now outsource their physical training, yet the principle remains the same."

"And you're all—orphans?" Sven said, brow furrowed.

"Indeed, all of us!" Demetrius confirmed enthusiastically. "The Most Worshipful High Cleric provided us with a home, guided us towards following the footsteps of the one true Sven, patron of street urchins and waifs. And he has now achieved an even grander feat: he demonstrated to us all that you, the one true Sven, are real. He resurrected you. All praise to the Shatterfist."

"All praise to the Shatterfist," the others chanted in unison.

With a sigh of resignation, Sven admitted to himself that he was stuck with these unusual fanatics for the foreseeable future.

The High Cleric, evidently eager for his turn to query, rasped, "Now, onto my question. Your current abilities correspond to an F-Rank level, yes?"

Shrugging, Sven replied, "Appears so."

The Cleric's countenance twisted into a scowl of dissatisfaction. "That wasn't my intention. I had hoped for the return of an S-Ranked warrior, as befitting the legacy of the one true Sven."

"Alright. Well, sorry to shatter your expectations. I didn't sign up to be here in the first place."

Ignoring the Cleric's grumbling, Sven shifted his focus. His patience was wearing thin, and he yearned to break free from the underground dungeon and focus on finding his way back to his family. The group's behavior, treating him like a prized horse, was starting to irk him.

"Why did you summon me to this world, anyway?" he asked. "Just to affirm my existence, or...?"

"Oh no," the High Cleric responded, his hands rubbing together in anticipatory delight as if he'd been waiting for this precise moment. "Fate has brought you here to serve us."

CHAPTER 9: BINDING SUMMONS

"Serve you?" Sven responded, feeling heat rise up in him. "You know you could have just asked. You're lucky Ash isn't here to hear any of this, you all would really have it coming then."

He sighed and let his hand drop.

There was a pause, and then Demetrius piped up, "Are you alright, Most Worthy Sven?"

"Oh, I'm far from alright!" Sven exclaimed, his voice echoing around the cavern.

He pointed an accusing finger at the High Cleric. "You brought me here against my will, expecting me to be your pawn, to serve you? I think not."

With that, Sven crossed his arms over his chest, his face set in a hard line. The rest of the robed men exchanged baffled glances, their faces a mixture of shock and confusion. As for the High Cleric, the old man simply watched Sven, his gnarled hands twitching as if itching to weave a spell.

"Oh, you find this amusing?" Sven taunted, his voice dripping with sarcasm. "Is this how you treat everyone you summon? As an indentured servant?"

"No, Most Worthy Sven, we're looking for a—"

The High Cleric cut him off.

Sven had a sinking sensation in his stomach for what this was all about. There was no doubt in his mind what that old bastard was waiting for. Yet, he already knew how this would play out. Since the High Cleric was the one who summoned him here, he would dangle the offer of returning him to his family, as a bond for his good behavior. This wasn't the first time Sven had been coerced. His fists clenched so hard the pommel of his sword dug deep into his skin. He needed more answers and throwing a tantrum right now wouldn't help him.

He straightened up, feigning a sense of calm

he did not feel. "Perhaps I misunderstood. What exactly is it you're asking of me?"

He waited. His chest tightened and his stomach churned as the old man paused, a gleam in his rheumy eyes. The old man finally straightened, aware of his audience, a smug smile playing on his lips, clearly enjoying the turn of events.

"We need you to protect this world. You, the one true Sven," the Cleric declared. "Who else is better suited for such an important task?"

Sven took a deep breath in and exhaled noisily. It always came down to some kind 'end of the world' deal with damn cultists. He processed it and moved on. The trick would be to decide to go along and feel angry about it… or dig for more answers. He needed to say something he'd been silent for too long. "Are you serious? Where are the great heroes of today?"

"Who better to take on an important task than a god among men?" the Cleric said, his voice raised. *He was definitely enjoying this.* "We're the Sons of Sven. You're our devoted godfather of the order. Shouldn't you want to take care of us? Protect this world?"

"No!" Sven bellowed, scandalized. "And I'm not

your grandfather! I don't even know you people and you dragged me here against my will. Why would I want to take care of you?"

"Hm," the High Cleric scowled. "Not even for my orphan boys?"

Sven looked at the hooded figures and they looked back at him hopefully. "Sorry, lads. I'm no god. And I'm my own man. By using coercion it goes against the principals I stand for."

"I didn't want to resort to this. But everything I've learned about you convinces me, this is the way to go. Never fear, boys," the High Cleric said, raising his hands. Some of them shifted on their feet nervously. " He needs a touch more persuasion, let us guide him, shall we?"

Sven barely had time to react before the Cleric's palms met, and a tingle started to grow in the pit of his chest. Almost immediately, he felt a strange weight materializing around his neck. His hands flew to the source, fingers meeting a cold, hard chain. *This is what the damn quest meant.* He thought impotently.

"I'm not your puppet," Sven yelled trying to remove the chain. He wouldn't be controlled by anyone.

He grasped the chain and gave it a forceful

pull, hoping to snap it off. Yet the chain, cast from stronger magic than his abilities could handle, held firm. It did not yield, but Sven could feel the tension beneath his grip. His muscles tensed as he strained against the persistent magic.

For a moment, a flicker of hope ignited in him as he felt the chain waver under his strength. But it was short-lived. The chain flared up with an ominous, crimson light and tightened its grip. Yet, Sven didn't wince, didn't scream. He stood his ground, challenging the Cleric in a test of wills.

"I'll ask again, will you comply?" The Cleric's voice was no longer smug, instead there was a steely resolve beneath his tone.

"No," his gaze locked onto the Cleric, unyielding.

Unfazed, the old man clapped again, and the chain's grip intensified. This time, it felt as if a vice was being clamped around his throat, cutting off his oxygen. He staggered momentarily, fighting against the sudden lack of air.

"Yield yet?" the cleric asked, a clear note of resolve in his voice.

But Sven, stubbornly shaking his head, responded with a barely audible but determined, "No."

Sven's world started to blur at the edges. The chain tightened further, blocking any vestige of air from reaching his lungs. His legs began to falter, but he fought the urge to kneel, pushing through the growing weakness.

However, even the strongest warriors have their limits. As the relentless grip of the chain persisted, Sven's vision started to swim, his strength gradually failing him. His steadfast refusal to surrender was being choked out of him, literally.

"That's enough!" Demetrius intervened, a note of pleading in his voice. "He's our namesake. We shouldn't treat him like this. Sven, please, will you help us?"

The moment the Cleric lifted the spell, Sven sprang into action, sword ready. But the Cleric was prepared, a fourth clap echoing off the stone walls and Sven found himself brought back to his knees by the restrictive chain, his sword clattering to the stone floor.

The spell lifted, and Sven rose, a visible struggle but he managed to keep himself upright. His breaths came in ragged gasps, and he was slightly swaying, but his spirit remained unbroken. The chain, a stark reminder of his current predicament, was still wrapped around his neck, pulsing with power.

A chuckle escaped Sven's lips, a low and menacing sound echoing around the room. He rose to his full height, his eyes reflecting the dim light, piercing through the murky shadows with a dangerous glint.

"I don't take kindly to coercion," he growled, his voice a rough echo in the cavernous space.

His hands, calloused from many battles, clenched into tight fists at his side. "You've chained me, yes, but don't think for a moment that it makes me your dog."

The Cleric met his gaze, unrepentant and solid in his conviction. "I do this for the greater good, Sven the Shatterfist. If this makes me the villain, I will take that role. Do not think I take pride in forcing you. But my children's lives are at stake and I will do *anything* to make sure they survive what is coming. Including forcing you with this chain… if that means I pay with my life or you end up choking me with it if you escape, I am prepared to take that risk."

The air thickened with tension as Sven took a menacing step forward. "Don't tempt me, old man," he warned, the threat hanging heavy in the air. "I've broken stronger chains than this."

A ripple of discomfort passed through the hooded figures, their once stalwart beliefs seeming to waver. They glanced at each other, suddenly unsure. Sven's reputation was not one to be taken lightly, after all.

"And if this chain should break," Sven continued, his gaze unflinching as he held the cleric's eyes, "I assure you, I won't hesitate to make you regret ever summoning me."

The High Cleric, however, didn't falter. He merely nodded his head his lips solemn. "I have no doubt you will try. You wouldn't be Sven the Shatterfist if you didn't try."

Despite the situation, Sven had to admit, the old man had courage and determination. Even if it was misguided. The old man was motivated, oddly, that loosened his own anger. He took a deep breath through his nose and stared

"Now what?"

CHAPTER 10: MEMORIES STIRRED

The High Cleric raised his face in supplication, his skin luminescent in the dim light, eyes almost completely white as some... power filled his body. "A hero's duty awaits, Sven," he said, voice hypnotic and whispery. Something within Sven knew these words held meaning, almost prophetic. "Our world teeters on the brink of annihilation. An infernal grand duke, Abaddon, lays waste to all in his path. This world will crumble under his vile reign unless someone halts his conquest."

Sven, rubbing his arms to hide how the small hairs had risen, under the guise of restoring circulation, shrugged dismissively. He was still angry and unwilling to concede anything. "Sounds like a rough deal, I'll give you that. But I fail to see where I come into this picture."

The Cleric's shoulders slumped, his face weary and tired. "Because even the system seems to agree that you are our best choice." he retorted. "You'll comprehend soon enough. Fetch me some water, boys."

At his summons they scuttled to comply, Sven noted their panicked inefficiency with an embarrassed wince. He recalled the school he and Ash had set up at Castle Twilight and understood an eager youth. After a few moments of their fruitless searching, the Cleric sighed, his patience evidently worn thin. A snap of his fingers and a sizeable basin filled with water appeared.

Sven quirked an eyebrow. "Why send them scrambling if you could just conjure it up?"

"Even an old dog needs to see his pups run, Sven," the Cleric said. "Moreover, my magic isn't as inexhaustible as it once was. Summoning you here took a considerable toll. It's a delicate balance."

Sven remembered Ash's magic draining away during their encounter in the Kingdom of White Lions. He winced, the memory still sore.

"Peer into the water, Shatterfist," the High

Cleric instructed, his tone tired and implacable.

Reluctantly, Sven complied. The basin's surface began to swirl with the Cleric's conjuration, the spectating hooded figures crowded closer. Their excitement was palpable, though, it made him feel strangely cornered.

"Behold," the Cleric whispered. "Your future, should you refuse us."

Sven gazed into the basin. Darkness unfurled, punctuated by brief, stark flashes of light. Screams of terror echoed as the vision descended into bedlam.

"What is this?" he demanded, fear creeping into his voice.

"Patience, Sven. Clarity will come."

Suddenly, he was standing in a field at the start of winter. Green pines covered in a light dusting of snow encircled him. The ground beneath still showed signs of life, and winter winds whistled through the trees. However, he felt no chill. Nothing. He glanced downward to find his feet hovering just above the frostbitten earth.

Then, the world around him started to change. It sped up, the frost and desolation grew heavier, thicker, like a world trapped in perpetual winter. The once evergreen forest was now a skeletal reminder of its past glory . The sky above him a perpetual twilight, devoid of the warmth of the sun. It was a world drained of warmth, of hope and life.

The world blurred and now he was near civilization. Like a ghost, he traveled. Cities lay in ruins, their towering structures nothing more than crumbling silhouettes against the bleak horizon. Streets that once thrived with life and laughter were now filled with an eerie silence, broken only by the whistling winds. People wandered aimlessly, their faces devoid of hope, their bodies mere shadows of their former selves. Their emotions, the bleak despair, battered at his will. He grit his teeth trying to keep such dark emotions from drowning him. He placed a mana barrier around his mind in the hopes it would at least ease the bombardment. The images were relentless.

He witnessed the downfall of kingdoms, the end of dynasties, the extinction of species. He saw nature wither and die, rivers running dry, and mountains crumbling. He saw hopelessness and despair, etched on the faces of all those who survived.

Sven staggered back, gasping for air. The

vision was overwhelming in its intensity, searing the harsh reality into his mind. It was an apocalypse, the end of all he knew and held dear. The world he'd just seen superimposed itself over the flickering shadows of the cave. It had been a grim picture of death and decay, a silent scream echoing in the void.

"Push forward, Sven," the High Cleric instructed, his eyes gazing at Sven in understanding, mouth dipped in sorrow. "You need to see more."

Sven gritted his teeth. As angry as he was, this superseded his personal feelings. He'd saved this world before and it *was* his birth place. Allowing that type of destruction when he could stop it, wasn't really in his nature. Before he was chained, he'd felt the old familiar excitement and joy as he fought against the dungeon. That sense of being *home*. Irrespective of how he was forced here, leaving his family behind—deep down, Ash would have wanted him save the world. *God he missed her.* She should have been by his side. Mentally shaking himself, he moved to lean forward once more. The icy field greeted him again. But this time, it was no longer silent. The ominous sound of snapping branches and heavy breathing permeated the air.

Something was approaching, something terrified.

A child exploded from the treeline. His face a canvas of fear. Muddied tears streaked down his cheeks, hair in disarray. The sight made Sven's chest tighten, the boy's frantic demeanor reminding him of his own daughter, Kaleigh, in her younger years. The boys' fear and the similarity to his daughter when she was younger, broke past his mental mana barrier and the kids emotions flooded over Sven.

"Over here, kid!" Sven bellowed, but the spectral boy didn't respond. Instead, he fell, and his ragged breaths filled the silence. Sven could feel his anger rising. He was a warrior, he was the Shatterfist, and yet he could do nothing but spectate. The feeling of helplessness started to claw at him. Especially when the boy whimpered and rolled over to look back where he'd been running from.

A new figure emerged from the treeline. An enormous, grotesque beast, bearing the head of a bull, massive paws of a lion and a mouth dripping with blood. It wielded a gnarled club, festooned with menacing spikes.

"Surrender, boy," the demon roared, its deep

voice resonating through the frigid air. It moved forward, catching the boy easily and raising him high above its open maw. Sven roared in frustration, lost to the sensations the boy experienced. Fear, despair and a plea for anyone to save him. The chains of the vision bound him tight, allowing no intervention. Not that Sven was coherent enough to understand that. He was captured within the vision, trapped as much as the young boy was.

Sven could tell the creature was savoring the moment. The demon let the boy drop, pinning him under one gargantuan paw.

"Gotcha," the beast growled. "You led a good chase, boy, but all games must end. Will you serve willingly, for eternity?"

The boy's defiance shone bright. "Never! You ugly cow-face!" he shot back, flinging a frozen clump of earth at the demon. Yet, the beast simply laughed, extending its claws threateningly.

"One last chance, boy. Serve me or face a fate worse than death."

As the child fell silent, Sven's heart pounded. He was the boy and understood the boy's fear; it was the fear of a prey cornered, a fear he had never personally experienced until now.

Without another word, the demon forced the boy to look into its fiery eyes. A gust of foul breath later, the boy's eyes turned vacant, a chilling emptiness replacing the fire of defiance.

The demon chuckled, carelessly flinging the boy aside. The child fell motionless, a puppet with its strings cut. His fear, his defiance, his life itself stripped away. With it, the emotional connection with the young boy disappeared too.

"Turning kids into mindless undead," Sven muttered, the weight of the revelation threatening to crush him. The demon's laughter echoed in his ears, the image of the child's vacant eyes seared into his mind.

Sven's mind couldn't help but replace the vacant eyed boy with his own daughter, Kaleigh. From her vibrant eyes and wild hair, to her unrestrained laughter at the simplest jokes and her tactful interaction with patrons at their local diner. The thought of his own flesh and blood facing a demon like this twisted his stomach into knots. He thought about the boy, someone's child, now a lifeless shell of his former self. His thoughts went to the parents. *Were they even aware of their child's fate?*

"This... this is not right," Sven grumbled as

the beast dragged away the zombie-like child. "It's utterly wrong."

A hoarse voice echoed in his ear, "So you agree?" The owner of the voice was none other than Demetrius, who yanked him out of the horrifying vision.

Back in reality, Sven found himself amidst the hooded figures in the dim-lit cavern. His head swam, akin to the aftermath of too many mugs of strong ale. The High Cleric's aged face loomed over him, uncomfortably close.

"Give the man space, will you?" Demetrius waved at the others, the respect in his voice evident. "He just surfaced from a vision."

The men stepped back, creating a circle around Sven. The High Cleric, however, continued to lean over Sven, his crow-like eyes glinting—searching. Eventually, Sven retreated, pushing himself against the far wall.

"So, will you help us then? Will you heed our request?" the Cleric asked. "Will you aid us in defeating this demon? Save our city, our world?"

"You don't think you could have asked me for help another way?" Sven retorted, tugging at the chain around his neck.

The Cleric sighed, it echoed in the cavern, "Not

particularly. Your stubborn streak makes you a wild card. I needed reassurances you would help, even if the methods were less than honorary."

"This isn't over between us. But I'll help." He replied.

Sven heaved himself onto slightly wobbling legs. As he towered over the Sons of Sven, the vision of the child trapped with the demon caused a twinge of annoyance to pulse within him. He needed space. There was a gnawing urge to break away from the oppressive gloom of the cavern, to distance himself from these self-proclaimed followers of his legacy. They *supposedly* revered him, yet, there was a lingering, grating undertone that rubbed him the wrong way no matter how much he tried to discard it. In his eyes, he felt nothing more than a foot soldier for their cause. They were more interested in the ideal of him rather than the reality, and that's where the sticking point got beneath his skin.

He eyed the High Cleric. He was a manipulative old man, and went to great measures to get his way. Sven couldn't help but question the truth of the vision, the possibility that the Cleric was manipulating him for purposes he didn't understand. He would need to question these other members further. Perhaps Demetrious would be a good candidate to start with.

It was time to focus, Sven he chided himself, he couldn't do anything about his suspicions right now, *First things first, survive this dungeon, deal with this demon… then the Sons.*

Drawing a deep breath, he curbed his annoyance, focusing it instead on the tasks ahead. Memories of other times he had to bite his tongue came to mind, like with the drunks he had tossed out of the Rustic Grill back on Earth when they got too rowdy or tried to get handsy. Somehow, their poor manners seemed marginally more bearable than the High Cleric's company.

However, he knew his duty. If the vision held even a shred of truth and a demon was rampaging, he couldn't stand idly by. That was a level of evil he couldn't ignore, even if it wasn't his world anymore, although he he'd fought to save it in the past. It was most likely the reason the Cleric summoned him in the first place.

"Damn it," Sven muttered. He couldn't help but feel embroiled in this battle, whether he liked it or not. As an expert warrior, it seemed he had no choice but to do the right thing. With a deep breath, he steeled himself.

Faster than expected, the High Cleric was at his side, his yellowed teeth bared in a rictus smile of congeniality. "Excellent," the Cleric's voice rasped out like sandpaper on wood, "it is beneficial to both of us."

Sven shot him a sidelong glance, his temper flaring. "Beneficial? How in the world is this benefiting me? All I want is to return home."

"Ah, but lad, you have youth once again. A chance for a fresh start, a do-over of sorts. It's an opportunity I never received," the Cleric replied, his voice filled with an odd note of nostalgia. "Yes, I've had a long, fulfilling life. But just look at my state."

Sven bit back a retort, the old man's words sparking a raw nerve. He didn't wish for youth. He had never requested it. All he desired was to remain in his world, his haven, with his family.

Yet, an insidious voice inside his head questioned his very conviction. Hadn't he reveled in the thrill of the fight? Hadn't it felt exhilarating to be his old, formidable self again?

Banishing the intrusive thought with a shake of his head, Sven turned his gaze back to the Cleric. "And you just had to drag me back as a rookie? Not even a veteran, an A or B class, but a novice?"

The Cleric shrugged dismissively. "Your dormant abilities are there, most likely. Unlocking them, however, will be your own task. Now, it is high time we exit this dreary place and return to the world above. I suspect we have overstayed our welcome within the dungeon. Boys, could you assist the Shatterfist to the city?"

With an eager step forward, Demetrius volunteered, "It would be an honor, sir. Sven— I mean, the Shatterfist—"

"Call me Sven," Sven interjected.

Demetrius nodded, "Sven, it is. Please, accompany us. We'll aid you in settling into the city, perhaps offer a tour, and get to know each other."

The others fell in step, forming a semi-circle around Sven. He suppressed a groan, foreseeing an incoming barrage of queries about his past escapades. After the energy-draining hours spent battling creatures, and more so from the vision, he was in no mood for a storytelling session.

"Just a handful of questions," Sven warned them, his tone firm. "I'll entertain only a few, and once I say it's over, it's truly over."

An excited murmur spread among the Sons of Sven. Questions poured forth like a torrent, swirling around the adventures of his past, his youth, his compatriots. They probed, careful yet persistent, about Ash, their curiosity piqued by the stories of their time together and their disappearance. Inevitably, the questions shifted d toward the almost mythical tales of his death and rebirth, their fascination apparent in their wide-eyed stares as was the stories of the monsters he'd once fought.

Once the curiosity of the hooded men was somewhat satiated, the High Cleric intervened, his voice slicing through the lingering chatter. "Before you venture forth, allow me to equip you properly," he said, making the vision bowl dissipate into thin air with a deft flick of his fingers. "That weak weapon of yours will not suffice. Here."

As he spoke, a brilliant light enveloped Sven's Ancient Blade. When the light receded, in its stead was a serviceable steel longsword. Its form was simple, unadorned yet finely crafted. The Cleric surveyed the weapon with a hint of satisfaction in his eyes.

"The basics lad. This should be plenty for someone of your caliber," he added briskly.

Before Sven could blink, a sturdy shield materialized in his grasp and armor replaced and fitted itself onto his body. Like the sword, they were unpretentious in design, yet their quality was undeniable. Sturdy enough for any combat situation he might encounter, they were indeed a considerable improvement over his previous gear.

The Cleric, taking a moment to appreciate his handiwork, nodded in approval. "Good luck," he intoned, his voice echoing ominously in the cavern. As the shimmer of the newly forged equipment faded, Demetrius cleared his throat, stepping forward once again. His gaze settled on Sven, sincerity burning in his eyes.

"Sven, there's something else," he began, his voice weighted with gravitas. "We, the Sons of Sven, have long held a decree, a grand commandment that we've carried through the ages. It is our guide, our mandate. We call it the Grand Quest Commandment."

A collective nod rippled through the group, their shared dedication evident. Intrigued, although quite amused at the grandiose name, he couldn't help but tilt his head to the side. Despite himself, Sven found his interest piqued.

"And what is this Grand Quest Commandment?" he questioned, studying their faces.

Demetrius' eyes glinted with fervor as he recited, "It calls for the extermination of unslayable beasts that threaten the realms of men."

The solemnity of the moment was disrupted as Sven burst out laughing, a genuine, hearty laugh that reverberated through the cavern. The Sons of Sven watched him, their expressions a mix of confusion and mild concern.

"Apologies," Sven managed, wiping a tear from his eye. "It's just... this commandment of yours. It's quite something."

The truth was, their Grand Quest Commandment stirred a memory, a moment from his own past that felt light years away now.

"Grand Quest to slay the unslayable?" He chuckled, shaking his head as the vivid memory played before his eyes. "I've had some experience with that. I imagine your quest comes from the one I once put up when the Adventurer's Rest was mine. A quest to slay a dragon. That beast had killed a good friend of mine."

"And who was this friend?" Demetrius asked, his curiosity piqued.

His lips quirked into an amused smile as he reminisced. "A rather unique character... Rabbit, the Brave. I hung a portrait of him in my bar... although, he was more than a rabbit. According to him, he was a cursed dragon prince turned into a rather... lewd rabbit who traveled with me as a bard. He was a *terrible* singer."

A collective gasp echoed around him, but Sven was far away in his memories, his thoughts filled with mischief, laughter, and the strains of a lute that never quite hit the right notes. Rabbit, despite his quirks, had been a cherished friend, and had driven Sven to challenge the impossible once.

Perhaps, he mused, these Sons of Sven were not as far removed from him as he had first thought.

CHAPTER 11: PROMISED MEAL

A steady trudge led them through the shadowed cavern, up along an incline that promised the fresh air of the surface. As Sven moved, he felt a subtle weight lift off his shoulders. The High Cleric's implacable presence was a fading memory, replaced with the mild intrigue that the Sons of Sven invoked.

"What's with the ceremonial attire?" Sven shot a sideways glance at their flowing robes, a smirk twitching at the corner of his mouth. "You guys don't wear this getup into battle, do you?"

A snort of laughter escaped from Demetrius. "For rituals only," he clarified, his broad hand patting the heavy robe. "Imagine trying to fight in these. We'd be tripping over ourselves!"

"Right," Sven agreed, his smirk broadening.

The echo of their voices filled the cavern, and Sven found himself oddly drawn to these dedicated individuals. They were enthusiastic, eager, and ready to risk their lives for a cause they wholeheartedly believed in.

"We've dedicated years training under the High Cleric," Demetrius continued, pride echoing in his voice. "Aiming to mimic your combat style, as the legends have described. It would be an honor if you could assess our skills."

Robin, who had initially met Sven with skepticism, piped in, "Your Adventurer's School is renowned. We managed to get our hands on some sacred texts and studied your techniques relentlessly."

"Did you now?" Sven raised an eyebrow, a sense of nostalgia stirring within him. *He remembered the eager faces of his young recruits, their fiery determination to master the rigorous training.* It brought a warmth to his heart knowing his teachings had traveled across time, even if it was cloaked in layers of myth and religious fervor. "I would be interested to see those manuals, how they've been interpreted."

Nodding in understanding, Demetrius replied,

"We can arrange that for you. And don't worry about any further monster encounters. The ones we fought were...practice targets. Not implying you'd be concerned. But just to assure you."

A chuckle rumbled in Sven's chest. "I wasn't worried."

Despite the oddity of their worship, Sven found himself appreciating the sincerity of the Sons of Sven. Their origin stories, as orphans, tugged at a part of him that was all too familiar with abandonment and solitude.

"Looking forward to the manuals," he confirmed, curiosity piqued. This whole situation was bizarre, but the idea of his legacy carrying on—albeit twisted in the stories and worship of a strange cult—held a certain appeal. And now, he was intrigued to see how his teachings had morphed across the past forty years.

The notion of manuals for survival techniques being revered as sacred texts intrigued Sven. The mundane turned divine in another world—it was a comical thought.

"These sacred texts," he mused aloud, "Are they full of grand prophecies, and cryptic wisdom?"

Demetrius chortled, shaking his head.

"Nothing of that sort, I'm afraid. Just practical combat strategies, survival tips, basic monster lore, things you'd probably find mundane. But to us, they represent the essence of the Shatterfist, a revered chronicle of your teachings."

If Sven's guess was right, these texts, manuals essentially, contained the distilled knowledge he had once imparted to his novice adventurers - nothing more than basic survival tips and combat strategies. Yet, in this world, they had been elevated to a sacred status in accordance with his legendary persona

A wave of mixed feelings washed over him - pride, amusement, and a touch of disbelief. It was flattering and disheartening. Flattering because they studied his techniques and therefore his legacy did live on—disheartening because for such basic tenets that made him wonder what happened to his prior students and where the latest S-Rankers were. The prospect of seeing these 'sacred' manuals also intrigued him. Sven couldn't help but wonder how much of his original teachings remained and how much had been lost or twisted in translation over time.

"Looking forward to it then," Sven affirmed, his mind full of curiosity. It would be interesting to see which survival tips and combat techniques had evolved into sacred scripture and why. Regardless, his adventure had just begun.

As they navigated the convoluted network of tunnels, the young man named Demetrius threw back his hood, revealing a youthful face. A head of unruly blond hair and an off-center smile were the two primary features Sven registered. The lad was reminiscent of Montesquieu, a noble-born recruit he had trained years ago. Perhaps there were universal traits among youths, regardless of the era they resided in.

"I will go collect them," Demetrius responded, catching Sven's attention, "and have them delivered to your quarters."

"My quarters?" Sven echoed, not having given thought to his lodging arrangements. An innate part of him assumed he would be left to fend for himself.

Catching onto Sven's hesitation, Demetrius hastened to clarify. "We've arranged for you to stay in the Room of Honor at the Sons' Chapel. But if you'd prefer otherwise..."

"No, that will suffice," Sven interrupted, "And don't forget those manuals."

Their journey through the labyrinth of

passageways continued in silence. With each step, they ascended subtly, and gradually, the gloomy corridors began to lighten. *Perhaps an indication they were nearing the surface.*

Robin finally broke the silence, casting a hesitant glance towards Sven. "I know you must be weary, but could you demonstrate some of your battle techniques at some point?"

His sentiment was echoed by Demetrius, "We've made assumptions about your fighting style. We would love to have them validated by you."

Sven responded in a gruff tone, "First, let's get to the surface. After that, I don't mind showing you some moves. But I have one condition. You have to share with me the lore of 'Sven' in this era."

The request was met with awkward glances exchanged between the Sons.

Demetrius was the one who responded, "Honestly, Shatterfist, some of it might sound quite... outlandish."

"That's precisely why I wish to hear it," Sven shot back with a smirk, "I could use a good laugh after the day I've had. You owe me at least that."

Somewhat taken aback, Demetrius yielded, "Fair point. While you might not have wished to cross over, we truly appreciate your presence...and we're sorry about that chain. We debated heavily about using it, but the High Cleric was insistent it was needed and he had the final say."

The other Sons echoed this sentiment with a chorus of approval. Sven sighed internally. *There was no point worrying about it now.* Looking at the eager faces he found it hard not to reciprocate their enthusiasm. These lads were not that different from his former trainees, despite their affiliation with a strange cult, in his honor no less.

Finally, they turned a corner and were suddenly in a narrow passageway with small dusty windows high on the walls. It was more like a basement than a dungeon, and when they approached what looked a lot like the back of a cupboard Sven furrowed his brow in confusion.

As they paused before the odd cupboard, a few yards behind Sven, a hushed conversation between two Sons caught his ear.

"He's actually taller than I imagined," one voice murmured, a note of awe creeping in.

"I heard that he once rode a Hydra into battle," the other replied, the reverence in his tone betraying his belief in the myth. "Do you reckon it's true?"

The other shrugged. "No idea, but we have to trust in the One True Sven. Even when the tales talk about a speed test running against monsters."

Sven found himself suppressing a chuckle at their earnest speculation. These tales about him seemed to get more outrageous by the minute.

As they ascended the stairs, the hushed conversations of the Sons carried over to him. Some fragments of their discussions perked his ears. One voice commented, "His eyes are sharper than the tales suggest," to which another chimed in, "And did you notice his hands? They say he once strangled a Basilisk bare-handed!"

The sheer imaginative extent of these rumors was impressive, making him smirk at the wild tales. No doubt, his persona was amplified by years of storytelling and had become more of a myth with each telling.

Due to the strange events of the day, Sven was physically drained. The battles he had fought, in addition to the mental exhaustion from the surreal revelations, took a toll on him. He hid a yawn behind his hand, hoping his weariness didn't appear too conspicuous. Fortunately, the Sons seemed to intuit his need for rest.

"Allow me to show you to your room," offered

Demetrius, stepping forward swiftly. "Dinner will be prepared later in the hall. You'll have the opportunity to meet the rest of the brothers."

Robin, his eyes still filled with curiosity, asked, "Would you consider showing us some of your combat techniques?"

Sven studied the lad for a moment, then asked, "Is there a training ground here?"

Robin nodded enthusiastically. "Yes, outside, in the back."

"Then, after dinner, I will," Sven agreed. "But let's not forget our arrangement. I'm eager to hear your tales."

Demetrius had a faint blush on his face, but he nodded in acknowledgement. They navigated through the wine cellar, winding up a slim set of spiral stairs made of stone. With each door they passed, some of the Sons veered off, leaving Sven and Demetrius to continue their ascent.

Sven, despite his exhaustion, felt curiosity bubble up within him. "What about the old man, the Cleric. Will he be joining us for dinner?"

Demetrius grimaced, hesitating before he answered. "The Most Worshipful High Cleric typically dines alone in his quarters, in accordance with his status."

"Is that so?" Sven questioned a hint of disapproval evident in his voice.

During his time running his training school, he made it a point to share meals with his students. It fostered a sense of community and allowed him to stay connected with the younger generations, an aspect that he believed kept him youthful.

"Well..." Demetrius conceded, rubbing the back of his head sheepishly, "on occasion, he does join us. For rituals, feast dinners, and such. But for the most part, he keeps to himself. His duties require a great deal of his time."

Sven hummed noncommittally in response, leaving the youth visibly nervous.

"I understand your reservations," Demetrius began, taking a step back. "You were brought here without your consent, and you've had to adjust to this world. The Most Worshipful High Cleric has his peculiarities, but his intentions are good. He believes you're the world's only hope, Shatterfist. The demon Abaddon poses a grave threat, and your power is our best chance to fight back."

"Abaddon's has done the unforgiveable, I can't argue with that," Sven replied, his thoughts returning to the vision he'd seen earlier.

Demetrius paused in front of a door on a small stone landing adjacent to the staircase. He produced a set of keys from his robe and handed them to Sven. "This is your room, and these are your keys. The larger one is for the room and the smaller for the wardrobe inside. Dinner is three floors down, in a room similar to this one. We usually gather around seven. You should find everything you need in there. We've prepared it for you, hoping our summoning would succeed this time.

"And I'll remember the manuals," Demetrius added, the anticipation evident in his voice. "I'll bring them to you later."

Sven weighed the keys in his hand, unlocking the door as Demetrius watched. He doubted he'd be able to keep the Sons out, but it was worth a try to regain some semblance of privacy.

As the door creaked open, Demetrius shuffled awkwardly. "I'll leave you be, then."

Once the youth was out of sight, Sven closed the door behind him and attempted a locking spell. His hopes faltered as he felt the magic surge within him only to dissipate into nothingness. Not only was the system and it's supposed upgrades different, but the fundamentals were different; his magic wasn't the same here. Certain spells worked while others didn't. He'd need to figure out the why of it later.

Sven examined the room: spacious, furnished with a comfortable bed and a large wardrobe. He used the small key to unlock the wardrobe, revealing clothes in his size. Shaking his head at the bizarre thought of his measurements being a part of ancient lore, he proceeded to check the rest of the room.

Large windows allowing ample daylight and a bathroom with a large copper bathtub made the room feel welcoming. He drew a warm bath. His eyes widened in appreciation when he saw more accoutrements and added some lavender bubble bath. Inhaling, he let the calming scent envelop him. He was a captive here, albeit in rather comfortable accommodations.After his bath, Sven donned a plush bathrobe left on the door and then pulled on loose pants. He closed the window shutters to darken the room and crawled into bed for some much-needed rest. It wouldn't be long before he had to face the Sons again, this time in a less formal setting. For now, sleep was his only desire. As for the dinner, and whether the High Cleric would make an appearance, that was yet to be seen.

Sven slipped a hand behind his head as he lay down on the large feather bed, sinking slightly into its soft comfort. He found himself staring blankly at the ceiling, his mind teeming with thoughts. Amidst all the strangeness and danger he had been thrown into, two faces emerged from the whirlpool of his thoughts—Ash, his wife, and Kaleigh, their daughter.

He could almost see Ash's warm smile, the way her eyes sparkled with laughter, and her soft hands that had often comforted him after a long day. Then there was Kaleigh, who was growing up to be every bit as clumsy as her mother.

But as he lay there, in this room prepared with such consideration by strangers who admired him, Sven found the silence... soothing. The solitude offered him a break, an unexpected reprieve from the continuous battles and obligations that came with his reputation. The room's comfort, the luxurious bath, and the promised meal created...*comfort*. A haven he needed just to gather his thoughts. He felt a pang of guilt mixed with his relaxation.

They won't hold it against me if I'm enjoying this just a little, he thought to himself, as if hoping the sentiment of his words would carry to his wife and daughter. Ash, ever understanding and wise, would probably smile and tell him he deserved it. Kaleigh, with her youthful enthusiasm, would laugh and demand he tell her all about his adventures.

Sven ran a hand over the cool, crisp sheets on the bed. The realization that he was a world away from his family, in an era that revered him. It was overwhelming. And yet, in the quiet of this room, he allowed himself a small indulgence of contentment, a rare feeling he hadn't experienced in a long time.

With one last thought for Ash and Kaleigh, he allowed his eyes to flutter closed. His last thoughts before sleep claimed him were of them. He'd face whatever this world had in store for him, and he'd fight with all his might. But for now, he allowed the luxury of the room and the silence of the moment to sweep him into a peaceful slumber.

CHAPTER 12: FIRST APOSTLE

Sven's eyes snapped open. He took a moment to take in the unfamiliar surroundings, the dim light seeping through the closed shutters, the absence of Ash's comforting presence. He sighed. The reality of the situation washed over him like a cold wave.

"There's no Ash here" he muttered, hoping against hope that he'd hear her soft reply. But the only answer was silence. He was alone in this strange new world, trapped in a youthful body and an unwilling guest of the Sons.

He was pulled from his thoughts by a loud knock on the door. "Dinner in ten," Demetrius called out. "If you're still joining us."

A faint smile tugged at Sven's lips. "Sure. I'll be

down in a few."

The sound of retreating footsteps echoed through the silence, but Sven didn't rise immediately. His mind was already plotting, examining his situation. He might not like his options and dining with the Sons, well, they didn't seem too bad. Regardless, he was not powerless. Unaware of the world and the recent politics he may be, but he was not powerless. Technically he wasn't truly a prisoner either. Even with the chain hanging over his head, he was more than capable of escaping and the High Cleric needed him to cooperate when he wasn't around to hold his chain. So there were more options. However…it was his *honor* that chained him.

"No one will shackle me. I won't allow it," Sven murmured, *not even myself,* he thought grimly. He focused his will, reaching out to the unseen threads of the enchantment that held him captive in this new world.

He could sense the magical chains wrapped around him, restricting his movements, his powers. With a surge of defiance, he tugged at them, testing their strength. The enchantment wavered under his strain, its grip slackening just a fraction, but it held strong. There was just something... different about how it worked. Connecting with the spell felt like oil floating atop water. His will was the oil and the spell the water. The two worked side by side, but separate at the same time.

Yet, the tiny victory was enough for Sven. It was proof that the enchantment was not unbreakable, that he had a fighting chance. And Sven was a man who knew how to make the most out of any opportunity. He would continue to resist, to fight, until he broke free.

Throwing open the shutters, he let the daylight pour in, banishing the shadows. He dressed quickly, donned his cloak, and descended the staircase. He arrived at a door where the torchlight flickered invitingly, accompanied by the sound of excited chatter. Stepping through, he entered a large hall, void of windows but buzzing with anticipation.

"Shatterfist!" Demetrius hailed him, a note of relief in his voice. "Over here!"

Sven's eyes fell on the enormous table at the center of the room. He suppressed a low whistle. It was laden with an impressive feast: a piglet roast with an apple in its mouth, steaming loaves of brown bread, a stuffed turkey surrounded by an array of winter vegetables, and pitchers of ale placed strategically at every spot. His stomach growled in response. It had been a while since he'd eaten a proper meal.

"The legends told us you liked ale," Demetrius said, a note of anxiety in his voice. "So we made sure to have plenty of it. And we set out all our best feast foods. We didn't know what you might want to eat, and—"

Sven placed a comforting hand on the boy's shoulder, cutting off his nervous ramble. "It looks great. Let's sit down and you can tell me some of these legends."

Demetrius glanced at the empty seat at the head of the table. "I don't think the High Cleric is coming. He hasn't said anything—but he usually shows up by now if he's planning on joining the meal."

Sven hid his satisfaction behind a nonchalant mask. A meal without the unnerving presence of the High Cleric was a bonus. "We'll all miss him," he said, feigning disappointment. "But you can let him know that I understand." *No point poking the bear this early.*

Relief washed over Demetrius's face. Sven guided him towards the head table. His mind was already on the roasted pig, but he couldn't shake off the feeling of being watched. His instincts had kept him alive in countless battles, and he wouldn't ignore them now.

As they settled down for the meal, Sven kept his senses alert. He was far from home, surrounded by strangers. It would be foolish to let his guard down. He would need to stay vigilant. Tonight, he was not just Sven Shatterfist, the hero. He was Sven, the prisoner, and soon he would plan his escape.

"The Blind Prophet is one of my favorite parts of your legend, Shatterfist," he blurted out, his voice ringing clear in the hall. "Basequin was your first true apostle, wasn't he?"

His question hung in the air, a palpable expectation thrumming amongst the Sons, their eager eyes fixed on Sven. The moment, brimming with their anticipatory silence, enveloped Sven, briefly stifling the noise of the bustling feast. It was clear how deeply they held onto the narratives of their hero, their faith unwavering, their belief in him unshakeable.

For a split second, Sven grappled with himself. Their hopeful faces gazed upon him, as if his story, however distorted it might be, gave them a sense of purpose, an idol to look up to in their otherwise bleak world. He found himself torn between setting the record straight and sustaining their uplifting spirits.

Looking at the food Sven's stomach rumbled so, once he'd heaped a plate high with food and poured himself a generous pint of ale, he turned to the closed group of Sons.

"All right. I want to know what you think I've done?"

He took a big bite of turkey and stuffing as the lads looked around at each other nervously, then washed it down with a swig of good beer. It was delicious—especially after a decade of eating diner food. He was proud of his cooking and of what he and Ash had built together, but there was nothing like a good feast day meal.

"Well," Robin said, "I can start."

The Sons at the other tables in the hall looked over eagerly at the prospect of a story, and Sven motioned them over. They seemed younger then the group of lads he'd first met in the dungeon—trainees, perhaps, or apprentices. At the far end of the room was a table full of children who seemed fresh from the orphanage they'd been found in.

Once the whole group was gathered around

the high table, Robin haltingly began his tale.

"They say that when you were young," he said, "not much older than some of us are now, you took a boat to the Near Islands and left your home behind."

"That much is true," Sven said, taking a big bite of pork and gravy. "I was a cabin boy."

"And there you met Basequin the Vibrant, the blind prophet, and you helped him to see again. You met him on the docks and he, with his power of second sight, knew that you would be the first fighter to vanquish him. He had never been beaten before. But his honor forced him to fight you anyways. Even though you were a green lad not much older than we are now, you defeated him.

Another of the younger boys rose off his chair and added, "'Lo!' Basequin said. 'This young boy has power greater than I, and I will serve him to the end of my days!"

Robin, giving the younger boy a dirty look continued on with his tale, "And the Shatterfist —by which I mean you—laid his hands on Basequin and cured him of his blindness. From that day forward the prophet followed you like a loyal servant, defeating evil throughout the Near Islands, driving back the forces of darkness as you drove the blindness from Basequin's eyes. At the end of your journey he sacrificed himself for you in battle, laying down his life out of love for you, and you soared on to glory elsewhere, a man grown. All hail the Shatterfist!"

"All hail the Shatterfist!" shouted the rest of the Sons, and Sven took an uncomfortable sip of his ale.

"Um," he said. "That's not really what happened."

Basequin had been a skilled fighter, and they had met in the Near Islands, but the arrogant young noble would never have agreed to be anyone's servant. He and Sven had been equals, fighting together, and Basequin had stayed blind until the end of his days. He'd died in battle—but not in glory, and not for Sven. They'd just been overmatched in a fight, and his death had been senseless.

He looked out at the Sons' faces, shining with joy that they'd finally met their hero, and thought about telling them all the truth. But...

I can't do it, Sven sighed.

The Sons were all orphans, and they must have taken inspiration from Sven's own story. While he hadn't been an orphan when he was their age—

Ma Riley had always been waiting for him to come home—he had gone out on his own and made a name for himself. He could see how a group of lads might take comfort in a story like his.

One of the Sons interrupted, his eyes full of reverence.

"The Blind Prophet is one of my favorite parts of your legend, Shatterfist," he blurted out, his voice ringing clear in the hall. "Basequin was your first true apostle, wasn't he?"

His question hung in the air, along with an expectation amongst the Sons, their eager eyes fixed on Sven. The moment, brimming with their anticipatory silence, enveloped Sven, briefly stifling the noise of the loud feast. It was clear how deeply they held onto the narratives of their hero, their faith unwavering, their belief in him unshakeable.

After a moment of silence, Sven looked up again, an idea suddenly taking shape in his mind. He raised his mug of ale, drawing all eyes to him.

"I'll tell you a tale of Basequin the...Vibrant you've never heard before," he began, his voice commanding the room. If Basequin were alive today he'd be demanding a duel for having his honor besmirched. To be given the title of *the*

Vibrant, he would have loved it... or hated it. He'd never believed in titles. An air of anticipation settled over the group as they listened, their collective breath held in suspense.

"Have you heard the one about the Sea Serpent of Trondel's Bay?" He asked, a mischievous twinkle in his eyes. Heads shook around the table, eyes wide, intrigued. Good. He had their attention.

"Basequin and I were still green behind the ears, but that didn't stop us from taking on any challenge," Sven began, his voice weaving an enchanting rhythm, captivating his audience. "Trondel's Bay was known to house a monstrous sea serpent, a creature as long as a ship's mast, with teeth as sharp as cutlasses and scales as hard as iron.

"They say the serpent was the scourge of sailors, sinking ships and feasting on the crew. It had been terrorizing the bay for months when Basequin and I arrived. We, full of youthful bravado, took it upon ourselves to rid the seas of this menace."

Sven took a draught of his ale, pausing for effect, relishing in the rapt attention of his audience. "Basequin was a born sailor, and he knew the seas like the back of his hand. He crafted a brilliant plan. We were to lure the serpent with a bait ship laden with barrels of the spiciest peppers from the southern isles.

"The plan was simple, yet daring. We would draw the serpent to the surface with the bait, and once it took a bite, the burning sensation from the peppers would drive the creature mad, forcing it to surface where we could attack it."

He spread his hands outwards, the orphans a captive audience. "And that's exactly what happened. As soon as the serpent took the bait, it went into a frenzy. It surfaced, thrashing about in the water, its scales glistening in the midday sun. And there, on that tiny boat, Basequin and I stood, ready to face the beast.

"With a harpoon in hand, Basequin took aim and threw it with all his might. The harpoon found its mark, embedding itself into the creature's eye. The serpent gave a monstrous roar, writhing in pain, but Basequin's throw had been precise. The creature, in its agony, retreated to the depths, never to be seen in Trondel's Bay again.

"As a token of gratitude, the sailors of Trondel's Bay gave Basequin a golden amulet shaped like a serpent, which he wore around his neck until the day he passed. And that, lads, is how Basequin the Vibrant earned his place in the annals of heroism."

A chorus of cheers erupted around the table; the Sons captivated by the story. Sven raised his mug again, taking another long sip, a subtle smile of satisfaction curling his lips.

Sven asked, his voice steady yet infused with interest, "Do you have another story you can share with me? I want to know more about my companions through your eyes."

Robin's face transformed, his lips splitting into an eager grin. "I do! The tale of Rabbit, Dragon Prince—"

Sven raised his hand, swiftly cutting him off, "Maybe not that one. Another, if you've got it."

Poor Rabbit's tale wasn't the kind of story Sven had the heart to hear now. It was filled with sorrow—the curse that morphed a noble dragon into a giant rabbit, the self-destructive life of exile, the disillusioned hope of regaining a lost kingdom, and the horrific demise in dragonfire. Such narratives were not what he needed.

"Understood," Robin stuttered, his youthful face shaded with disappointment. "Then, how about the tale of your departure from the world with a promise to return in its direst need?"

The boys listened intently, their eyes bright with anticipation. Sven offered a nod of approval and helped himself to more roast piglet.

In a voice that echoed throughout the hall, Robin began. "As years wore you down, your world was in peril. A voracious demon was ravaging the land, leaving naught but ruin. Amidst this chaos, you, who had retired to your school with friends and your loyal mage-servant Ash, believed your adventurous days to be over. No one would've faulted you for stepping aside. But, the world needed a savior, and you took up that mantle."

To Sven's surprise, Robin was weaving a tale that held a kernel of truth, though embellished.

Robin continued, his voice a mixture of admiration and sadness. "Though your mage-servant was deteriorating, and you weren't as spry as you once were, you charged headfirst into battle. The demon was a formidable opponent, and victory seemed impossible. Still, you fought tooth and nail. When hope was fading, you decided on a desperate plan—a potent magical attack that could take your lives along with the demon's. But, if it saved the world, it was a sacrifice worth making."

Sven swallowed hard at Robin's words. He remembered feeling old and worn, many of his friends already gone. The legacy he would leave behind was in the hands of the school. But Robin's rendition was a far cry from the harsh reality of his own memories.

"You cast the spell, but death did not embrace you. Instead, a portal to another world yawned before you and Ash, and you stepped through."

In that other world, Sven had found a new life—where he was no heroic adventurer, just a humble diner cook named Tom Riley, with a loving wife, Ashley, and a sweet daughter, Kaleigh. Despite the mundane existence, he had found a peculiar joy in his new life, leaving behind the blood-soaked past.

Before Sven could dwell on those memories, Robin chimed in, "But before you left, you made a solemn vow. You promised to return if our world was ever in need. No matter the circumstances, you'd find a way. Such is the Shatterfist way, the way of the One True Sven."

Sven looked at the eager faces around him, at the boys who idolized him. His past, his tales, his exploits—they gave these boys hope. He had carried many burdens, but this one felt heavy in a different way. He was not just a hero in their stories; he was their symbol of resilience and strength. And that, perhaps, was the most vital role he had ever played... and the heaviest chain.

Sven rose to his feet, the gleam in his eye replaced with something deeper, something fiery. He held his mug high above his head, his voice strong as he picked up where the sons had left off.

Robin's face beamed with anticipation as he made a grand gesture. "Actually, we put together a little something while you were sleeping, a new epic."

He produced a lute from somewhere behind his seat, strumming a few notes to check its tuning. From around the hall, other Sons took up various instruments—a hand drum here, a set of pipes there. They waited in expectant silence, the murmur of the hall falling away, as Robin began to strum a somber melody.

The Sons around the table joined in one by one, their voices rising in a harmonious chorus that filled the room with a resonant melody. They sang:

> "In the twilight of life, stood a warrior bold,
> With Ash, his mage-servant, loyalty untold.
> Their strength waned, their youth no more,
> Yet into the fray they bravely bore.

The demon they met, a foe most fierce,
Their blades and spells, its hide tried to pierce.
Victory, a wisp, just out of reach,
They battled still, a lesson to teach.

Hope seemed lost, the end was nigh,
In desperation, they turned to the sky.
A spell of great power, with lives as the cost,
To save the world, no matter the lost.

They invoked the magic, death's cold hand near,

Yet the Reaper's grip, they did not fear.

Instead of the end, a portal did appear,

And through it, they vanished, leaving all they held dear."

The Sons' voices fell silent, leaving only the echo of their song hanging in the air. The hall was quiet, every eye turned to Sven. "This is the new part we added tonight." Robin said hesitantly. "The High Cleric spoke about your world briefly." Sven nodded encouragingly.

"In this world new, no wars to be fought,

No more was he an adventurer, no foes to be sought,

Tom Riley he was named, a humble cook fryer,
A life of peace, was all he did desire.
With Ashley, his wife, a love so profound,
And Kaleigh, their seed, joy truly unbound,
His battles behind, a past life of strife,
In this world, he had found a new life."

Once the noise died down, Sven held up his hands for silence, a sly twinkle in his eyes. "Now, that was quite the tale, lads," he said, his voice still strong despite the laughter that had preceded it. "But I believe I did promise a different kind of story. One of my favorite tunes from my younger days. A tale about a lusty barmaid who had hearts aflutter across the land."

Sven started to clap a steady beat, his face splitting into a broad grin. "This one," he said, his voice rich with mirth, "is for all of you young men out there who think you've got the world figured out. Believe me, there's always a barmaid ready to teach you a thing or two."

And with that, Sven launched into a rollicking ballad, filled with clever wordplay and bawdy humor, about a barmaid who'd outsmarted a whole tavern's worth of braggarts and would-be suitors.

With the echoes of the tale still hanging in

the room, the Sons raised their cups in unison, a chorus ringing out, "All hail the Shatterfist!" Sven's grip tightened on his own mug, the cool ale doing little to wash away the vivid memories Robin's tale of his final adventure here, had stirred.

Visions of a demonic foe, a landscape marred by devastation, and his faithful friend, Ash, weakened and fading, danced before his eyes. They had survived, true, but the memory was a weighty one, nonetheless.

He scanned the room, meeting the eager gazes of the Sons, their faces painted with anticipation. They were waiting, he realized, for a response.

Breaking the silence, he found his voice, "Indeed, lads, that's how it was. Now, who's up for learning some moves? I'm offering training."

A cheer went up through the room as the Sons scrambled for their swords. Sven seized the opportunity to down the remnants of his meal, his mind eager for the physical distraction of training.

Led by Demetrius, they filed through a small door at the back of the hall and emerged into a snug stone-walled training yard. The darkness of the evening had fallen, and the torches affixed to the walls came alive under the lad's practiced touch. The familiar sounds of city life echoed in the background.

Robin's voice broke through the noise, "Apologies for things being so loud. Busy street."

Sven asked, "So we're in a city then?"

Demetrius replied, beaming with pride, "Largest in the kingdom. The yard may be cramped, but we manage. We often clear out the hall and make use of it when we need extra space. The High Cleric is understanding."

Nodding, Sven took a longsword from the rack, its location shielded from the weather by a slight overhang. "Good to know. Let's get to some katas."

As he led the Sons through a series of katas, Sven felt a familiar ease wash over him. His body remembered the sequences of his youth, and the Sons, quick to learn, were soon moving in sync with him. The shared rhythm, the focused energy —it felt like being back at the school.

Yet as Sven found himself immersed in the practice, a glint from the Sons' building drew his attention. He glanced up to see the High Cleric observing them from an upper floor window, a inscrutable look etched on his face. Sven couldn't help but wonder what lay behind that stern gaze.

CHAPTER 13: A MAN IN HIS ELEMENTS

For the next hour, Sven devoted himself to molding the Sons, honing their raw skills and abilities. He initiated the training session with basic katas, seamlessly transitioning into more complex forms, his movements sharp and precise. The lads followed suit, their mimicry of his movements an echo of the past, albeit a less polished one.

The first kata was straightforward—the Rising Sun, a sequence of basic attacks and defenses meant to warm up their muscles and acclimate them to the rhythm of combat. He watched as they moved in sync, their arms flowing and feet stepping to an age-old dance of martial prowess.

Next, they moved on to the Serrated Edge, a sequence that tested both speed and precision. The katana was designed to cut, not bludgeon, and Sven demonstrated how to land clean, efficient strikes. The Sons followed along, their faces screwed up in concentration as they sought to mimic his motions.

Some of the Sons were impressive in their talent, their movements sharp and decisive. He could see the fundamentals of his old teaching within their style, a distant but tangible link to his own school. His gaze darted from one Son to another, a wave of recognition passing over him. They had been learning from him, indirectly.

The final drill was the Dancing Wind. It was a flowing, continuous kata that blended offense and defense into one smooth sequence. It was a test of endurance, skill, and focus. By the end of it, Sven found himself panting slightly, a thin sheen of sweat coating his brow.

But he was satisfied. By the time he called for the end of the training session, the Sons were gasping for breath, their faces flushed with exertion. They had improved, even within the span of an hour. It was undeniable that they'd had access to his teachings. He was a believer.

"Good work, lads," he said, sheathing his weapon. He glanced at them, their faces flushed with effort, chests heaving. He had to admit, despite the strangeness of the situation, he found himself filled with a sense of accomplishment.

The echo of his own teachings was alive within them. They carried a part of his legacy, however they had come by it, and Sven found himself looking forward to the next training session. This was a chance to correct, improve, and perhaps even evolve his own teachings through these eager young warriors.

The sense of satisfaction that washed over Sven was quickly replaced with a burgeoning determination. As he regarded the panting, sweaty forms of the young warriors before him, he knew it was time to push them even harder. They had displayed commendable aptitude in their swordsmanship, a testament to their diligence and the impact of his teachings.

"Alright, lads!" he called out, clapping his hands together to gather their attention. They straightened, their chests heaving with exertion as they turned towards him. "You've done well with the katas, but now we move on to physical conditioning. This is what separates the men from the boys."

Despite the groans that greeted this announcement, Sven was unyielding. He led them through a grueling session of physical training, demanding push-ups, running in place, up-downs, and then even more push-ups. The courtyard echoed with the sounds of grunts, gasps, and the scuffling of feet on stone.

Their expressions varied from determination to dismay as Sven pushed them past their perceived limits, ignoring their grumbles and complaints. It wasn't about punishment or hazing, it was about discipline and endurance. As a warrior, the state of their bodies was as important as their skill with a blade.

The training grew more intense, their bodies straining against the unrelenting exercises. Sven didn't let up, pushing them with the ferocity of a drill sergeant. His commands echoed in the confined courtyard, bouncing off the walls as the Sons complied. Their breaths came in ragged huffs, bodies slick with perspiration under the cool night sky.

Sven could see their resolve wavering, the tempting allure of surrender flickering in their eyes. But he also saw determination. They were fighters, and this was just another battle to win. Their resilience was a beacon, a shining symbol of their commitment. It was proof enough they could withstand the trials of the path they chose to walk.

"Come on, lads!" Sven shouted above their heavy breathing, "The road to strength isn't an easy one, but by the gods, it's worth it!" His words, though stern, carried an undercurrent of pride. These were his students, his legacy. And they were proving themselves to be worthy of that honor.

After the taxing session, Sven allowed his gaze to drift towards the Cleric's window again. The aged man was no longer observing, his silhouette absent from the glass. A sense of relief washed over Sven; the intrusive scrutiny had left a sour taste in his mouth. He reminded himself that this surveillance, a consequence of the chain around his neck, would persist as long as he lingered in this realm. This realization spurred his determination to escape with renewed vigor.

Demetrius was quick to extinguish the flickering torches as the training session concluded, their intense glow diminishing to a few dying embers. The young warriors dispersed, their faces glowing with a victorious exhilaration that was testament to their hard work.

"The finest bout yet!" Robin exclaimed, a youthful vibrancy lacing his words. "Would you consent to more?"

"Perhaps," Sven replied, softening his tone. "But our time is constrained, isn't it? You summoned me for a reason."

"But could you not remain here? With us?" The young man's voice was desperate.

A single word echoed in Sven's mind. *No*, But he didn't say it out loud.

"I have a realm to return to," Sven explained. "That's where I belong. As you have your place, so do I."

Robin's countenance fell at his words, yet he offered no further protests. Sven ascended the staircase towards his resting quarters, his mind a whirlwind of thoughts. He had to constantly remind himself; these boys, as enthusiastic as they were, were not his responsibility to bear.

Exhaustion claimed him swiftly once he lay in bed, yet sleep did not offer solace. His dreams were plagued by haunting visions of Kaleigh. He saw himself in pursuit of her through a flower-dotted field, her laughter echoing as she evaded him. The child held a simple bouquet of dandelions and despite his best efforts, he failed to catch up. The nightmare took a disturbing turn when she revealed an aged visage that mirrored the High Cleric's. Her laughter transformed into a malevolent cackle that jolted him awake, leaving an unsettling echo in his ears.

As he lay in bed, mulling over the haunting dream, the door swung open abruptly. The High Cleric ambled in, prompting Sven to pull his blankets closer, shielding his disheveled state.

"What!" Sven exclaimed, startled by the sudden intrusion.

"It's time," the aged Cleric rasped. "You've had your merriment, Shatterfist. A good bonding with the lads. But your purpose here extends beyond that. It's time to fulfil it."

"My purpose is going home, if helping you gets me there, so be it," Sven replied, trying to maintain his composure. "But could I be granted the courtesy of getting dressed first?"

The Cleric dismissed Sven's protest with a wave of his hand. "Tomorrow, you shall venture into the first dungeon. But today, familiarize yourself with the city. Get acquainted with the people whose lives hang in the balance, pending your success against the demon. Learn to cherish this world again, Shatterfist."

Sven felt a sense of anger rise up within him at the Cleric's words. There was an undercurrent of permanence in his tone, as if the possibility of Sven's return to his world was less likely than not. The Cleric's disregard for his eagerness to go back home only served to fan the flames of Sven's resolve to find his own path back.

He nodded. "Sure. I'll get dressed, find some breakfast and explore the city. Sounds like a plan."

The Cleric scrutinized him, as if he was trying to guess what was on Sven's mind. But without further comment, he turned and shuffled out, leaving Sven by himself. As for Sven, he waited, ensuring no prying eyes were spying on him before he rose from the bed and approached the window.

He flung open the shutters, revealing a bird's eye view of the largest city he had ever seen. The Sons resided in a towering structure, central to the bustling city. Below, citizens hurried along the streets, their movements an echo of the same urban life Sven had been avoiding on Earth. Merchants haggled, carriages trotted along, and the general air of the city felt more chaotic than what he was accustomed to.

Despite his desire to leave, his curiosity had been piqued and he wanted to go explore the city a bit.

Sven quickly dressed and made his way downstairs. The hall from the previous night was deserted, but the alluring smell of bacon guided him into the kitchens. A handful of the young warriors were huddled around a less imposing table, devouring their breakfast.

"Shatterfist!" Demetrius exclaimed, prompting the boys to look up. "Can we serve you anything? More tales, or--?"

Sven shook his head. "The Cleric has other plans for me today. But I'll take a bacon and egg sandwich to go, if you don't mind."

A young lad quickly cracked two eggs onto a sizzling pan, while another, armed with a sharp knife, sliced a soft roll and placed it over the grates of an ancient wood stove. A short while later, a deliciously fried sandwich was carefully encased in wax paper by a third boy.

His expression was shy, yet his eyes radiated with admiration. "Hope you'll return soon," he said, his grin revealing a pair of missing teeth. "Watching your moves was...cool."

"Thanks, lad," Sven replied, gently accepting

the warm package. He turned to Demetrius, "Could you point me towards the exit?"

Guided by Demetrius, Sven soon found himself standing in front of the imposing front doors of the Sons' tower. A twinge of guilt surfaced as he looked at the neatly packaged sandwich. The boy had put in effort, and he was about to hastily consume it on some street corner. Well, the thought was what counted, he supposed.

Once the towering doors had swung shut behind him, he eagerly unwrapped his breakfast. The sandwich was a delightful blend of perfectly toasted bread, eggs cooked just right, and a hint of salt and pepper for the extra kick. The young chef had done a commendable job. He devoured the sandwich, letting the burst of flavors provide a momentary distraction from his situation.

Finishing his meal, Sven focused his attention on his surroundings.

He was tucked in a narrow cobblestone alley, shadowed by the intimidating structure that housed the Sons. The building was a stone fortress, its stature significantly dwarfing the neighboring buildings. Sven observed the street, the familiar cobblestones and odd structures, and his gaze fell upon tall posts crowned with glass globes, reminiscent of the electric lights in Ash's world.

Streetlights in any world were practical, just in Ash's world, there were more.

Curiosity led him closer to one of these posts, but with the daylight and the lights off, there was little he could discern. Thus, he journeyed down the alley, finally spilling into the thrumming thoroughfare.

His eyes scanned the multitude of faces as they passed him, their eyes occasionally flitting to him with curious interest. The Head Cleric had stated that he'd learn to love these people and this world again, but could he?

The attire here was different—men garbed in formal three-piece suits and women adorned in elaborate dresses and boots. All dressed predominantly in shades of black and gray, the somber colors contrasting against the vibrant energy of the city.

Sven felt out of place in his casual attire, nothing close to the refined suits worn by the city's men. As he navigated the bustling streets, the odd looks from the passersby confirmed his feelings of being an outsider. It was a discomforting reminder that he was far from home, in a world that he hadn't called his own in a long time.Dismissing the curious gazes and whispers, Sven focused on exploring the new city.

The sheer scale and hustle of the place dwarfed anything he had previously known. He was aware that Ash's world contained cities exponentially larger than this one, but he'd never visited them. Comparatively, this city was an intimidating sprawl next to his familiar Kingdom of White Lions.

He missed his home. The Rustic Grill, their warm restaurant, the sound of Kaleigh's laughter; a wave of regret washed over him. But he silenced it, focusing on the present.

"Chin up, Sven," he muttered under his breath, mentally rallying himself. *One step at a time*.

As the day inched towards noon, he finally stumbled upon something familiar: a humble tavern with a charming red door, a wooden sign swaying gently in the breeze. The sign read, "The Blind Goat".

As he reached the tavern, Sven murmured to himself, "Time for some familiar ground." He took a deep breath, hand on the tavern door, before entering. He sighed in relief. No matter where a person went, a tavern was still at tavern. A small drink, it was still quite early and some hearty food sounded like the perfect idea right now. The fact that this location was sufficiently distanced from the intrusive High Cleric was an added benefit. The Sons themselves were actually growing on him. A quick scan of the street confirmed he wasn't being tailed, so he pushed the door open, stepping into the welcoming warmth of the tavern.

The tavern was mostly deserted at this hour, save for a few elderly patrons nursing their drinks. The bartender, a wiry individual with a weathered face, looked up from his task and gave Sven a nod of acknowledgment.

"Make yourself at home," he gruffly gestured towards the vacant stools.

Taking the man up on his offer, Sven crossed the room to take a seat at the bar, its wooden surface worn smooth by countless patrons before him.

"Could I get a pint of ale, please?" Sven requested, settling onto the high stool.

"Light or dark?" the bartender asked, already reaching for a mug.

A smirk tugged at the corner of Sven's mouth. Yes, this was his kind of establishment. The simple choices reminded him of his days at the Adventurer's Rest, where he and Lloyd had experimented with numerous brews. Nowadays, he preferred things uncomplicated.

"Dark, please. And do you happen to serve shepherd's pie?" he asked.

The bartender stared at him as though he had suddenly sprouted an additional head. "What kind of tavern would we be if we didn't have shepherd's pie?" he grumbled, shaking his head.

Sven's hearty laugh echoed through the nearly empty tavern as a grin split his face. He leaned back on his stool, the worn wood creaking under him. "An empty one, I'd wager," he responded, his eyes twinkling with good humor. "Just like a blacksmith without a hammer or a bard without a tune." His words were met with a smattering of chuckles from the few patrons present.

The bartender's stern expression cracked, replaced with a grin matching Sven's. "Well said, stranger. I'm Matthew. You've got the spirit. Shepherd's pie it is, then."

Filling a tall mug to the brim, Matthew quickly disappeared into the kitchen to begin the shepherd's pie. Sven took the opportunity to find a comfortable spot at the bar, his mind wandering to thoughts of escape, the chain around his neck the only thing reminding him of his current predicament.

His pint, rich and full-bodied, delivered a satisfying kick. When the shepherd's pie arrived, warm and delectably seasoned, it was a comfort that was much needed. Matthew, having delivered the meal, busied himself with washing glasses, the silence comfortable between them.

Eventually, Matthew broke the silence. "You're obviously not from around here, lad," he said. "What's your business in Westville?"

Sven blinked at the 'lad' reference, momentarily forgetting his restored youth.

"Just passing through," he answered casually. "Got some work lined up."

"And who might that be with?"

Sven looked at him directly. "Ever heard of the Sons of Sven?"

Matthew grimaced slightly. "Can't say I haven't."

Feigning nonchalance, Sven continued, "I'm here to teach them a thing or two in the kitchen. I run a tavern back home. Knew a couple of the younger Sons from there, so they roped me in."

"Is that so?" Matthew replied, a hint of interest in his tone. "You're a cook then? What's your specialty?

"Call me Tom. And I cook homely food. Think burgers, fries, even fried pickles."

Matthew's expression was one of bemusement, prompting Sven to stand. "Here, let me show you. If you're open to it, of course."

"You're welcome to give it a go," Matthew acquiesced, his tone taking on a hint of caution. "Just a piece of advice, though. Keep your guard up around the Sons. They're not to be trusted, any of them. They're zealots, cutthroats, and rogues, all wrapped up in one unsavory package."

Sven let out a chuckle at the bartender's words. "Not exactly the kind of people you'd trust with your silverware, right?"

Matthew's mouth twisted in a wry smile. "Sounds about right. Keep your wits about you with them. If you've got something they want, they won't hesitate to take it."

Sven's smile turned cold. He thought of the summoning binding spell on him and the demand to tackle a demon. Not to mention the heavy handed way the High Cleric went about getting his help. Sven also suspected the demon wasn't going to be the only 'evil' the Sons would want him to destroy. He suspected the High Cleric would try his best to 'utilize' his skills for his advantage. The

High Cleric struck Sven as a man who hungered for more in life. There was no denying that he was helping orphaned kids. But it wasn't for altruistic purposes. No, Sven suspected there was more that the High Cleric kept close to his chest.

"Thanks for the advice, Matthew," he said, his voice tight.

Matthew, catching his tone, decided to drop the subject. "Well then, once you finish your cottage pie, the kitchen is yours."

CHAPTER 14: OWN PACING

"Any other intel on the Sons?" Sven finally asked, finding Matthew's gaze.

Matthew threw a quick, nervous look around. "Let's talk in the kitchen. You were going to show me that...what was it?"

"Burgers and fries," Sven replied, washing down the last of his shepherd's pie with the remnants of his ale. "Got ground beef, salt and pepper, potatoes?"

"We have that."

Ketchup might be an issue, he thought. *Might need to make this burger taste good enough without it.* A hurdle, but nothing he hadn't faced at the grill.

Stepping into the kitchen, Sven was in his element. Even though he was in an unfamiliar place, this was familiar territory. He began to take stock of what he had to work with. "Just you watch, Matthew," he muttered to himself, "Let's see how you like 'simple' food."

Just like that, Sven was lost in the world of culinary arts, momentarily forgetting about the Sons, demons, and otherworldly missions. For the time being, he was just a cook sharing his craft.

Matthew fetched the ingredients, his voice dropping to a murmur as he began. "The Sons are a peculiar lot."

Sven raised a brow. "You don't say?"

"It's not just their peculiar lifestyle. Orphans living in a central tower, it's certainly unusual. They are capable fighters. And in these...troubling times, they've proven their mettle."

"The demon," Sven clarified.

Matthew's face tightened. "Yes, the demon."

"But they have been battling it, haven't they? Protecting the city?"

"That they have. Credit where credit's due. They've thwarted it and its minions time and time again. But their methods...they're questionable at times. The ends justify the means for them, if you catch my drift."

"I do," Sven acknowledged, quietly accepting

the potatoes Matthew handed over. His tenure with the Adventurer's Guild and his old friend Galen had exposed him to such types before. Life, he thought, certainly had a knack for bringing things full circle.

Setting to work, Sven warmed the oil, expertly peeling the potatoes and slicing them into thin sticks before submerging them into the hot liquid. Simultaneously, he formed the ground meat into a loose disc and placed it in a separate skillet with a bit more oil. As the food sizzled, the kitchen filled with the tantalizing scent of their efforts.

"Got any bread rolls?" Sven asked, glancing at Matthew.

Matthew furrowed his brow. "Like hot cross buns?"

"Never mind that. Any roll will do."

Matthew complied, and Sven toasted the roll to a golden brown, carefully turning the burger and stirring the fries as they cooked. The resulting dish might not be an exact match to the Rustic Grill's signature plates, but it was pretty damn close.

Suddenly, the kitchen door creaked open and an elderly patron from the bar peered in. "Caught a whiff of something delicious," he commented, his eyes lighting up. "What's cookin'?"

Sven flashed a warm smile. "You'll find out soon enough. I've made enough for everyone to sample."

The portions were modest, but no one would be left out. A few fries for each wouldn't hurt, either.

As the meal came together, Matthew passed Sven a large serving plate. The ease with which Sven plated the food spoke volumes about his proficiency in the kitchen. It was just like his combat skills; rehearsed to perfection, the actions were instinctive, almost subconscious. The techniques, once mastered, were forever etched in his muscles.

His entrance into the main room with the dish was met with eager anticipation. The patrons, mostly older men, looked intrigued by the unusual meal.

"What've we got here?" queried the man who'd first smelled the enticing aroma, his eyes surveying the food. "Never seen the likes of this before."

"Burger," Sven announced, "Give it a shot, it's worth it."

He carved a chunk from the patty, skewered

a piece of the toasted roll, and savored a bite to demonstrate. The rich flavor profile hit his taste buds instantly. The quality of the meat here surpassed any he'd encountered back on Earth. Even in the absence of ketchup or mustard, the savory flavor of the dish was unbeatable. The patrons were soon tucking into the meal heartily, their reactions to the fries was yet to come.

"Might need to source some ketchup for next time," Sven mused aloud, "that would elevate it to a whole new level."

Matthew intervened to clarify Sven's affiliation. "This guy's cooking for the Sons."

The ambiance subtly changed, a ripple of apprehension passing through the room.

"Those fellas," the first patron muttered through a mouthful of burger, "Can't trust 'em."

A second man countered, "They ain't all that bad. Saved our hides from the demon last time it showed up."

"That blasted demon will wreak havoc, just you watch," the first man retorted, cynicism dripping from his words. "And the Sons of Sven? Doubt they'll be the ones to stop it. They lack the power, and... they just aren't cut out for it."

Matthew interjected, trying to steer the

conversation away from the ominous topic as he sampled a fry, then another. "Can we not talk about the demon now? Feels like it's eavesdropping whenever we mention it..."

His words had barely faded when a shrill scream echoed from the street outside. As if on cue, Sven's hand instinctively reached for his sword.

With his gaze fixed on the door, Sven asked, "Do you think it's him?"

Matthew, distancing himself from the windows, wrung his hands in visible distress. "It always happens this way."

"Always?"

"Yes. No sooner do we utter a word about him than he arrives. Like clockwork."

Sven's brows furrowed. "That's peculiar."

A targeted naming spell, perhaps? A way to sow fear and unease amongst the populace.

"I'll check it out," Sven declared, making for the door.

One of the elderly men intervened, placing a restraining hand on his arm. "Too risky, lad. Stay put. Chances are, he won't bother coming in here."

Sven nearly retorted but remembered his appearance. No longer was he the weathered adventurer of old. Now, he was a seemingly inexperienced lad who had introduced himself as a cook. These folks probably thought he was delusional to even contemplate going up against a demon.

"I won't stray too far," he assured them hastily. "I'll just see if anyone requires assistance. With my sword, I can protect them and guide them here."

The first old man cautioned, "Just be careful not to lead the demon right to us, lad! We'd be nothing more than a breakfast meal to that thing."

"Maybe toss him the remains of the burger, see if that satisfies him," someone quipped.

Swiftly exiting the building, sword gripped tightly, Sven was greeted by the pandemonium outside. The cacophony of alarm bells resonated through the air as townsfolk scrambled in terror, clutching children or dragging carts laden with belongings. Reacting on instinct, he pressed his back against a wall as a frantic horse-drawn cart narrowly missed him. The poor creature was in a state of absolute panic, its eyes wide with fear, while the driver desperately tried to escape whatever was causing the mayhem.

"What are you doing, boy?"

Sven found himself facing a well-groomed

young man who attempted to brush past him, clearly taken aback when Sven didn't budge.

"I'm no mere boy," Sven stated, his grip on his sword hilt firm. "I'm here to offer assistance wherever needed."

A scoffing laugh escaped the man. "You? I assure you, this situation is beyond your capabilities, lad. I'd advise you to flee while you still have the chance."

Before Sven could articulate a response, the polished gentleman was on his way again, attentively avoiding anything that could potentially tarnish his immaculate footwear. Sven was ready to tail him when a bone-chilling shriek, followed by the sound of shattering glass, redirected his focus. Tracing the source of the commotion led him to the first henchman of the demon around the corner, leering menacingly at a little girl who was attempting to make her escape into a barricaded shop via a broken window. Her skirt had been ensnared by a piece of sharp glass and, in her panic, she struggled to free herself as the abomination neared.

The beast was a hideous sight, a nightmarish blend of wolf and man. Its lower half resembled a wolf's with hairy limbs tipped with razor-sharp claws, whilst its face exhibited grotesquely human features distorted by a large, snout-like nose and a set of piercing teeth. It seemed to take delight in the child's fear, growling at her while its mouth overflowed with frothy saliva. The little girl yanked at her dress, but to no avail.

The time for observation was over. Sword in hand, Sven sprang into action. His sudden attack took the creature by surprise, its eyes reflecting the shock as his blade attacked its first mark. With a swift, powerful stroke, he severed one of its muscular arms, spinning around to confront the beast as it responded with a rage-filled snarl.

"How dare you," it snarled, its speech hampered by its pronounced teeth and drooping tongue. "Who do you think you are, whelp?"

His patience was wearing thin with the repeated 'boy' label. Had he ever been so disregarded when he was an F-Ranker? It had been so long, he could barely recall.

Undeterred by its intimidation, Sven took an offensive stance as the wolf-beast lunged at him. His movements were guided by years of honed instincts as he sidestepped the creature's onslaught, swiftly countering with a decisive stroke of his sword. Despite lacking the might of Worldrender, his erstwhile weapon, this blade served its purpose well.

As the demon's minion collapsed in a lifeless heap, Sven rushed over to the little girl, carefully detaching her dress from the glass-strewn windowpane. He then gingerly picked her up, cautious of the shards, and placed her on solid ground.

"Thanks," she said, displaying composure far beyond her years… *he could relate*

"Are you unharmed?" he asked.

"Yeah. You aren't from here, are you?"

His brows furrowed. "What gave me away?"

"Such things happen often these days," she explained. "Most folks simply flee at the sight of these creatures. The spirit to aid others has been largely lost. We did try initially, but…"

Her voice trailed off into a quiet whisper.

"They just kept showing up anyways," Sven finished, trying to sound gentle. "And eventually the ones who tried to help faded away."

She shuddered. "Yeah. Faded away…or worse."

It sounded a lot like what had happened in his era.

"Let's get you somewhere safe," he said.

The little girl gave Sven a skeptical glance,

a reaction he found entirely reasonable. Who could blame her, given that the minions of the demon Abaddon had breached the town's safety? Nevertheless, he guided her down the streets, ruminating on a suitable refuge. The tower of the Sons was an option, albeit not his favorite. Yet it offered better protection than the exposed streets.

As if summoned by his thoughts, a group of Sons appeared, marching in their direction accompanied by a squad of men donning purple uniforms. The lead Son, a lanky, pallid boy with patchy skin, raced towards Sven at the sight of him.

"Behold the Shatterfist!" he announced with exaggerated enthusiasm. Instantly, the Sons and the purple-clad men stiffened to attention.

Sven resisted the urge to show his exasperation. This degree of deference was excessive, even by S-Ranker standards.

"Yes, I am the Shatterfist," he confirmed in a flat tone, barely concealing his lack of interest. "You've got that right."

"He saved me from that thing," the girl chimed in, pointing to the defeated demon creature.

They turned to witness the result of Sven's heroics.

"We've been trying to eliminate these creatures," the leading Son spoke, a note of disdain seeping into his voice as he eyed the fallen wolf-like creature. "Will you join us, Shatterfist?"

Sven responded with a nod.

"These gentlemen are City Agents," the Son elaborated. "I am Rogerton, leader of this team."

"City Agents?"

"In essence, city guards," explained the foremost man in the purple uniform, stepping forward and removing his hat with respect. "I am Richard Maxwell, the Deputy Head. We've teamed up for this mission. The Sons and the Agents."

"But under the direction of the Sons," Rogerton interjected, casting a hard stare at Maxwell. "We appreciate your collaboration."

Sven had little patience for the brewing power struggle between the two groups. Who took charge was of no consequence to him. Wasn't the city's welfare their primary concern? Why was this petty rivalry eating into the crucial time needed to defend Westville from the onslaught?

"Enough talk," Sven stated bluntly. "I suspect they're infiltrating from the east."

Rogerton responded with a nod. "The eastern gate appears breached."

"Then let's get moving and face these beasts," Sven declared, lifting his sword with a broad grin. "I'm quite looking forward to it."

CHAPTER 15: FOG OF BATTLE

Before Sven could join the Sons and the City Agents in their rush to engage the oncoming monstrous horde, a soft pull at his arm gave him pause. It was the young girl he had saved just moments ago, her voice a timid peep.

"Excuse me, sir... could you..."

Sven nodded in sudden realization. His thoughts had been so focused on the upcoming battle that he'd momentarily forgotten about her.

"Rogerton," he said, his gaze shifting to the stern man, "Can we send somebody to take this girl to stay in the Sons' Tower until the battle is over?"

Rogerton stared back at him, his brows knitting in puzzlement. "I beg your pardon?"

"Her. The child," Sven repeated, gesturing

toward the young girl. "It would be safer for her in your tower, wouldn't it? At least until we get rid of these demon things."

Rogerton's reply was a flat, curt, "No."

Sven's eyes widened in surprise. He was certain he'd misunderstood. "Excuse me?"

"No, Shatterfist," Rogerton repeated, his tone unyielding. "Our stronghold isn't some sanctuary that we can just open to anyone who comes knocking. If that were the case, wouldn't every single person in this city seek refuge there? We simply cannot accommodate everyone, and we certainly can't play favorites."

Sven was about to argue, but Rogerton held up a hand to silence him.

"Our rules may seem harsh, Shatterfist," he said, his arms folded firmly over his chest. "But they are rules nonetheless, and they exist for a reason. We are the Sons, not the Daughters. We have our orders, and we stick to them."

Sven's anger bubbled as Rogerton's callous words echoed in his mind. His fists clenched involuntarily, knuckles going white. Sven gritted his teeth, containing the seething rage.

"Rules?" he spat, "This is not about rules, Rogerton. It's about basic human decency! She's just a child. A child who should be protected, not left to fend for herself in these dire circumstances."

Rogerton simply shrugged, "We all have our parts to play, Shatterfist. Hers is to learn to survive."

"You know," Sven hissed, the intensity in his gaze sharp as he leveled it at Rogerton, "I have an actual daughter. I wouldn't dare dream of abandoning her in a situation like this."

Before he could respond, the young girl raced away from them, disappearing into the broken-windowed shop. Sven watched her go, a pang of worry tugging at his heartstrings. Rogerton simply nodded in approval.

"There's a lesson in that for you, Shatterfist," he said, crossing his arms over his chest. "In time, you'll see that the way of the Sons is the only way."

Sven's reply was cut short as the chain around his neck began to grow warm. He glanced down, eyes widening in surprise. The sensation was uncomfortable, but not painful. It was almost as if the chain was trying to tell him something.

Rogerton smirked at his reaction, clearly enjoying Sven's discomfort. "Getting used to it, are you?" he sneered.

Sven's expression hardened. "One day, Rogerton," he vowed, his voice a low growl, "This chain won't be a problem. And when that day comes, you're at the top of my list." *So, there were other 'Sons' within the order that preferred power over actually protecting people...This Rogerton would go on his shit list right under the High Cleric.*

With a final, seething glance at Rogerton, Sven forcibly wrenched his focus back onto the growing danger at hand. Amidst the turbulence of his own indignation, he knew he had a responsibility to uphold. Duty called, beckoning him to set his personal conflict aside and step up to the plate.

They delved deeper into the town square, with Sven leading the way. A heavy sense of foreboding descended upon him like a pall, the air seeming to thicken with each step. The scene that unfolded before him was a grim tableau of human terror and monstrous delight.Townsfolk huddled together like lambs to the slaughter, their faces etched with raw fear. They were besieged by the abhorrent snake-demons, their sinister bodies coiling and slithering.

"Alright, everyone!" Sven's voice boomed out, carrying above all the noise. He turned to face the frightened crowd, his grip tightening on the hilt of his sword. "I need you to stay calm, alright? We're going to get through this."

"Look at them, trembling in fear!" the largest demon hissed, its slitted eyes gleaming with cruel delight. "What should we do, brothers? Devour them now or set them free?"

"Devour them!" chimed in a smaller demon on its left, licking its lips with a forked tongue. "I've grown famished. They seem plump, too. City life has treated them well."

A third one weighed in, a thoughtful expression on its grotesque face. "True, but remember, Abaddon wishes to spread terror. If we feast on them all, who's left to narrate the horror that transpired here?"

A fourth demon, its belly audibly grumbling, chimed in, "Why not compromise? Devour half? Make a game out of it."

"An intriguing proposition," the largest demon agreed, its grin widening. "Let's select at random."

Their laughter echoed through the square as they began to discuss their selection process.

"What about every third human?" suggested one. "That way, we feast and yet, leave enough to spread our terrifying tale."

"Or maybe," another chimed in, pointing at a

trembling child. "We pick the youngest and the oldest. Show them we respect no bounds."

The largest demon tilted its monstrous head, considering the suggestions. "Ah, the cruelty of randomness does hold a certain charm. But feasting on the young and old..." it drawled, eyeing the child singled out by one of its cohorts, "that certainly sends a message."

"Or we could select by hair color," one demon proposed, its yellow eyes sweeping over the crowd, taking in the varying shades of hair. "Dark-haired ones first, then the blonds, then redheads... It'd be like a menu."

"Or perhaps we choose based on height," another chimed in, a wicked grin curling the corners of its mouth. "From the tallest to the smallest, or the other way around. Imagine the terror as they watch the pattern emerge."

"Why not let them choose?" a lean, cruel-eyed demon suggested, its grin razor-sharp. "Ask them to nominate who goes first. Pile the guilt onto their fear?"

The largest demon let out a thunderous, mirthless laugh, its tail thrashing in delight. "Now there's a game that could last the whole night!" it agreed, eyes gleaming with amusement. "Let's hear them beg and plead for mercy, bargain with their loved ones' lives. Let's make a spectacle out of it!"

As the demons debated their fates, the townsfolk pressed their backs against the nearest wall, their eyes wide with terror. In response, Sven's hand instinctively flew to his sword, ready to jump into the fray.

However, Rogerton raised a hand, halting him in his tracks.

"Stay where you're at, Sven," Rogerton advised, his tone suggesting a plan in the works. "I'm a mage. A well-aimed fireball should take out a majority of them in one strike."

Sven started to respond, "If you angle it correctly to hit only the demons—"

Rogerton had already turned, his focus trained on the task at hand. He extended his hands, conjuring a ball of blazing fire that hovered menacingly, three feet above the ground. Growing to about the size of a basketball, it then launched towards the cluster of demons.

However, instead of heading straight for the grotesque creatures, the fiery sphere started to drift towards the cowering townsfolk.

"No..." Rogerton muttered under his breath,

quickly casting a correction spell. Although the fireball shifted back towards the demons, it was too late. It collided with the mass, incinerating a few of the creatures but also dragging in three terrified villagers.

Astonishment and disgust replaced Sven's initially cool demeanor. "What was that?" he snapped, momentarily ignoring the chain around his neck. "What kind of sorcery was that?"

His mind wandered to Ash, his wife. She could have executed the spell flawlessly, harming none but the intended targets. The demons wouldn't have stood a chance against her precise magic.

Rogerton was clearly rattled, his gaze falling to the smoldering remnants of his botched spell. "It's a complex spell," he began, "The trajectory, the wind direction—"

"If you were truly a competent mage, you'd have factored all that in!" Sven cut him off, his voice seething with frustration. "Any battle mage worth their title—"

Richard Maxwell, the commander of the City Agents, interjected, his tone cool and measured.

"Shatterfist, it was an error. A tragic, unfortunate error."

"An error that cost innocent lives!" Sven

responded, his anger barely contained.

"But an error that also paved the way for others to escape," Richard countered, pointing towards the square.

Following his gaze, Sven saw the remaining townsfolk making a run for it. A ladder had been procured, and one by one, they scrambled up, seeking refuge on a rooftop. The last man to ascend pulled the ladder up behind him, eliminating any possibility of the demons following.

Maxwell's voice broke through the turmoil, practical and confident. "The townsfolk are safe for now, atop the buildings," he explained, gesturing towards the group above. "These demons aren't built for climbing."

Sven grunted, his gaze returning to the serpentine nightmares below. "Seems the mastermind forgot to add that feature."

Maxwell's eyes narrowed as he followed Sven's line of sight. "We believe Abaddon prefers a psychological strategy. He wants submission, not slaughter. Spends his resources corrupting the kingdom, instead of waging full-fledged war. Why shed blood when you can inflict fear?"

Sven frowned, his thoughts drifting towards

the innocent victims. "And children make for effective targets."

Rogerton, pale and shaken, nodded. "He's abducted a significant portion of Westville's children. Parents are paralyzed by fear. He snatches their children, and they're never seen again."

Sven's mind conjured the disturbing image shown by the High Cleric. "They become his servants."

"Correct," Maxwell confirmed, his voice hard. "We think he transforms them into those half-beast creatures. It's a terrible fate."

As Sven looked at Rogerton, his initial scorn softened slightly. The young mage was out of his depth, trapped in an overwhelming situation with seemingly insufficient guidance. Which reminded him...

"Where's the High Cleric?" Sven asked, scanning the area. "Shouldn't he be here?"

Had he been leading the Sons, he'd be at the front, charging into battle. But he wasn't the leader, nor did he aspire to be. He had to remind himself. His home, Ash and Kaleigh, awaited him. The Sons' dilemmas were their own to deal with.

"He usually monitors the situation from a

distance," Rogerton replied, his voice carrying a hint of defensiveness. "Back in the tower. But he keeps a watchful eye on us, rest assured, the High Cleric does more than his share."

Sven was about to retort, but a look from Maxwell halted his words. The message was clear: it was not the time for squabbles. There was work to be done.

Maxwell rose, gesturing to his agents. "Come on, we've got a battle to fight. There's plenty ahead of us today."

With that, they plunged into the depths of the chaotic city, cleaving through the monstrous horde with deadly precision. Sven noted the cohesion between the Sons and the City Agents; the result of numerous previous collaborations, no doubt. Their swift, methodical dispatching of the demonic invaders was impressive, but Sven's trained eye couldn't help but spot the recurring carelessness in Rogerton's magic, reminiscent of the disastrous fireball incident.

Memories of Ash's meticulous spellwork made the young mage's errors all the more glaring. Sven reminisced on Ash's dwindling powers during their time in the Kingdom of White Lions, her joy in wielding magic slowly giving way to desperation, culminating in her final spell: the portal back to Earth. Magic had been her life, and seeing her lose it was heart-wrenching.

Sven was jolted back to reality when a flurry of ice shards whizzed dangerously close over his head, missing their intended target and scattering uselessly on the cobblestones. "Watch it, Rogerton!" he barked, irritation lacing his words. "You're supposed to hit the demons, not your own side!"

"I'm trying!" Rogerton responded defensively, preparing another casting as a herd of bull-like demons charged at them. His hands moved in a frantic dance and another volley of ice shards flew out, panic etched on his face. The spell missed the mark entirely, narrowly avoiding hitting a couple of Maxwell's men who threw out a few choice expletives at Rogerton before refocusing on the onslaught.

Sven looked at Rogerton and, unable to hide his disappointment, shook his head. "Rogerton, control your magic," he advised, his tone carrying an edge of impatience. "Power without precision is like a wild beast—dangerous to all, including the wielder."

"But...but I..." Rogerton began, but Sven cut

him off.

"No buts, lad. Watch and learn," Sven stated firmly, a grim set to his jaw.

Around them, the street was filling up with a growing assortment of grimacing demons. Sven could sense the tide of the battle shifting in favor of their adversaries as Rogerton's botched spells continued to misfire. A sense of urgency coursed through him. Drawing his sword, he fell into a battle-ready stance, determination etching his features.

A duo of wolf-like demons locked their bloodshot eyes onto him. They advanced, grinning grotesquely, wielding oversized cleavers likely scavenged from a nearby butcher's shop. The creatures moved in a predatory manner, but Sven remained calm and ready. His years of battle-hardened experience taught him that timing was everything.

The demons came closer, their foul breath seeming to taint the very air around him... closer... their stained teeth stood out in stark contrast against their snarling maws... closer... their eyes, alight with malevolent hunger, locked onto their prey. As the demons entered his striking zone, Sven steeled himself, mentally prepared for the fight that was to ensue.

"Now, Rogerton, watch carefully," he muttered quietly, his focus shifting entirely to the approaching enemies. His hand tightened around the hilt of his sword, muscles tensed for the imminent battle. "Time to teach a lesson."

Sven dashed the remaining distance separating him from the wolf-like demons, his sword a silver streak in the fading light. A deft swipe, a twirl, and monsters crumbled onto the cobbles, life ebbing away from them.

"I am growing stronger," Sven thought, a newfound sense of power coursing through his veins. Perhaps his former abilities were returning to him, albeit slowly. While he was far from his peak as an S-Ranker, his prowess was markedly improved from the previous day in the dungeon.

Thrilled by the rush of combat, he let out a resonant battle cry, charging towards another contingent of demons. To his surprise and satisfaction, a handful of the Sons rallied to his side.

"I never dreamed I'd fight alongside the legendary Shatterfist!" exclaimed one, his eyes wide with awe and excitement.

The atmosphere hummed with electric

anticipation as another wave of twisted demons slithered out from the city's shadowy corners, their sinister gazes fixed on the group. Sven's impromptu band of Sons formed a protective circle around him, their faces reflecting a mixture of fear and determination. Sven hoisted his sword high, signaling the charge, and a primal roar echoed from the throats of the young warriors. Soon, the narrow city street was filled with the cacophony of battle, the harsh clash of metal upon metal ringing out.

Sven was a whirlwind amidst the chaos, his blade arcing through the air with lethal precision. Each movement was a dance, the rhythm of combat familiar and comforting. Despite the lack of his S-Rank abilities, his restored youth lent him speed and vitality. The Sons, while green and somewhat undertrained, fought with a surprising ferocity, taking cues from Sven and slowly pushing the demon horde back.

They have potential, Sven found himself thinking, even amidst the chaos. Yet he immediately pushed the thought aside. There would be no more training, no more guidance. Eventually, his path would lead away from this world—as quickly as his feet could carry him too.

The chaos of the battlefield continued to escalate. Demons lashed out at Sven's band of Sons, aiming to drag them down to the merciless stone street, but the young warriors held their ground. Sven caught them casting quick, uncertain glances his way, seeking guidance, reassurance. He nodded, acknowledging their courage, and plunged back into the fray.

A hulking bull-demon, dwarfing its brethren in size and ferocity, locked its bloodshot eyes on Sven. With a ground-shaking charge, it barreled toward him, its gore-soaked hooves kicking up debris. Sven met the creature's challenge head-on, his expression steely, his grip tightening on his weapon. As the demon lunged, he deflected the attack with a powerful parry, then retaliated with a blindingly fast thrust of his blade. The beast bellowed in pain as Sven's sword found its mark, its form dissolving into a dark cloud of smoke.

"Solid work, Shatterfist!" a nearby Son called out, his eyes wide with youthful admiration. Sven spared a brief moment to acknowledge him with a quick wave.

"You're holding your own quite well, too lad," he responded, his tone grudgingly admiring. The Sons fought valiantly, each member bravely defending the others. Their camaraderie was evident; they shielded each other in times of need, always ready to provide assistance. Even amidst the brutal combat, they showed no signs of backing down. Sven couldn't help but feel a growing sense of respect for these youngsters. They were standing tall under pressure, proving themselves capable, even in the face of adversity.

Submerged in the thick of the battle, Sven focused his attention on the stronger adversaries, leaving the Sons to tackle the lesser foes. He moved with the rhythm of combat, a seasoned warrior dancing with death itself.

However, even a seasoned warrior can be caught off guard. A flash of motion in his peripheral vision alerted him to a coming threat, but before he could react, he felt the thud of impact. The wolf-demon's club had found its mark.

CHAPTER 16: FORTUNE BE WITH YOU

The unexpected incident unfurled in a heartbeat. He was engaged in a swift exchange of blows with a sword-wielding snake creature one moment, and the next, he found himself staring down the harsh wooden reality of a club that was much too close for comfort.

Not ideal.

In the blink of an eye, the looming threat was no more. The club tumbled to the ground with a thud, the wolf-demon alongside it, life ebbing away, a dagger lodged firmly in its skull. And there, standing behind the fallen demon...

"Rogerton?" Sven blinked in surprise.

The lad barely acknowledged him, already back to concentrating on his struggle with ice spellcasting. *Huh, Rogerton might be more useful as a foot soldier than a mage. But he seems set on the idea that magic is somehow superior.* As Rogerton botched yet another spell, Sven sighed and plunged back into the mayhem.

The fight was a grueling one, but gradually, the Sons managed to drive the demonic horde back through the city streets, towards the breached gate they had entered from. The tide was turning in their favor. Cleanup soon became the primary task at hand, seeking out and eliminating the demons who had infiltrated deeper into the town, lurking within Westville's labyrinthine alleys.

"Let's spread out," Sven suggested once the intensity of the battle subsided. "Small teams, nobody goes alone. Let's comb through every part of the city, ensuring we've cleared all demons."

"I'll reach out to our other posts," Richard Maxwell chimed in, "We have Agents in every sector of the city. They can relay anything suspicious and assist in the cleanup."

Sven gave a curt nod of approval, then selected two young men—a Son and a City Agent—to accompany him. Richard Maxwell was someone

Sven could respect, a man reminiscent of many he had met before: concise, efficient, and competent. It was clear to Sven that, regardless of the world, City Guards shared a universal character.

As the group dispersed, Sven guided his small team into an alley that led to a small marketplace. There, they encountered three spidren demons mindlessly vandalizing an empty storefront, shattering windows with reckless abandon. He frowned at the needless destruction; there weren't even bystanders for them to terrorize, they were merely indulging their destructive urges.

The master behind these demons might be powerful, but he was definitely lacking in maturity.

If Sven ever crossed paths with this Abaddon—which he had a hunch might happen, considering the Sons' determination—he would make sure to give him a piece of his mind. And if luck was on his side, he might just be able to rid this world of his malevolent presence once and for all.

Upon hearing the telltale echo of their footsteps on the cobblestones, the spidrens swiveled around to face their unexpected guests. Sven's grip tightened on his sword hilt; the battle had been lengthy but not overly challenging by his standards. After years of monotonous diner work, he was actually quite primed for more action. Either Abaddon hadn't sent his elite troops for this mission, or he wasn't as formidable as the High Cleric had warned.

"Let's attempt a flank," Sven murmured to his young companions, his gaze locked on the disgruntled spidrens. "You go left, you go right. I'll hold their focus from the front. We should be able to clean this up quickly."

With a bit of fortune, they could be back at the Sons' tower, relishing some well-deserved ale and roast boar soon.

The Son and the Agent complied without question, encircling the trio of spidrens. The creatures emitted a series of hostile hisses and snapped their mandibles, their beady red eyes homing in on the new threat.

"Cease your interference," the bulkiest spidren demanded. "Let us ruin what we wish. In return, we will spare your lives."

Sven scoffed. He'd learned from a past betrayal never to trust a spidren. Deceit was in their very blood. "Not happening. If you dared to attack us, I think you'd encounter more resistance than you'd bargained for."

"Perhaps," the head spidren conceded, its gaze flitting between the three of them. "But we're merely smashing glass here. What harm does that do?"

"What about the owner of this shop?" Sven countered. "What will he come back to? His entire storefront ruined?"

A wicked glint flickered in the spidren's eyes. "Dead. I suspect he won't mind. His family too."

The gruesome words of the spidren ignited a fire within the Son and the Agent. They wore their rage like a banner, the intense emotions palpable in the way their knuckles whitened around their weapon handles. The spidren's revelation, steeped in crude nonchalance, did more than offend— it taunted their sense of justice and loyalty, a deliberate provocation.

Sven, recognizing the mounting storm, swiftly raised a cautionary hand. "Steady, lads," he cautioned, his voice a grounding timber amid the swirling chaos of emotions.

It was clear to Sven that the spidren sought to manipulate them, goading them into a blind rage to throw them off balance. Such creatures thrived on their opponents' reckless abandon, waiting for the opportune moment to strike down the unguarded.

Despite his efforts, his warning slipped through the cracks of their wrath. Their faces remained set, a storm of anger swirling in their eyes.

He exhaled slowly, a resigned thought forming in his mind. *Once again, it's up to me to keep the balance. As always.*

Later, he'd impart the wisdom of maintaining composure even in the face of harsh provocations. For now, the spidren had made it clear that talk was over. Action was required.

Gritting his teeth, Sven lunged at the nearest spidren. His sword sliced through the tense air, creating a lethal path aimed straight at the creature. It tried to lash out first and failed.

"Nice try!" he taunted, his every move an effortless dance of battle-honed skill. The spidren, taken aback, snapped its venomous jaws in retaliation. He darted sideways, his nimble feet carrying him clear of the potential harm.

"You'll need to do better than that!" Sven shouted out. Then, his sword swept out, cutting off one of the spidren's thin legs neatly at the joint.

A startled hiss erupted from the creature. It stumbled backward, its numerous eyes focusing on Sven with a newly kindled fury. He met its gaze unflinchingly, his resolve as sturdy as the sword in his hand.

The spidren hissed out an indignant retort. "You dare!" But Sven was already a step ahead. With the speed and precision honed over countless battles, his blade punctured its tough outer layer, carving a deep gash through its exoskeleton. Green lifeblood seeped onto the cobbles, the spidren collapsing under the fatal injury.

Still, he couldn't afford to pause. Two of the menacing beasts remained, closing in on him with a disturbing quickness, their hirsute bodies a blur in the dim light.

"Lads, to arms!" Sven barked the order, his voice carrying through the discordant sounds of their skirmish. The two boys, still aflame with fury, rushed in to provide support. Together, they engaged one spidren while Sven turned his attention to the remaining opponent. His sword weaved a confusing pattern in the air—left, then right—only to find the spidren unflinching.

"Ah, yes. Spidrens." Sven muttered.

A memory flashed in his mind, reminding him of the spidrens' deceptive nature. They were masters of guile, and therefore difficult to trick. A direct confrontation seemed inevitable.

You're overconfident," it taunted, its voice a grating chuckle that echoed off the surrounding buildings. "You're not as capable as you believe."

Sven just glared, "You'll see just how wrong you are."

The spidren snapped its formidable jaws, initiating a forward charge. Matching its aggression, Sven too lunged forward. He could see the surprise flicker in its multiple glowing eyes before they clashed head-on. The resonating clash of his sword against its razor-sharp mandibles sent a shower of sparks onto the cobbled street. The creature pushed against him, trying to overpower him with its brute strength.

Grunting with exertion, Sven pushed back, his muscles protesting against the strain. It was a bitter reminder of his diminished strength, a testament to the youth he had left behind. For a moment, the desire to reclaim that lost vigor overwhelmed him.

After a tense struggle, the spidren began to waver, releasing a furious hiss as Sven forced its head downward. He quickly retracted his sword from its jaws and delivered a swift, decapitating blow.

"That's down." He panted.

He glanced over to assess the situation of the two boys as they grappled with their foe. He stood ready to intervene if the fight took a dire turn. Much to his relief, they were faring well, their coordinated attack giving them an upper hand. The spidren was clearly thrown off by their teamwork, snapping aimlessly at one, then the other, unable to secure a target. It was a futile effort as the City Agent landed a decisive blow, causing the creature to slump lifelessly onto the cobblestones.

A moment of silence hung in the air before Sven voiced his approval, his eyes still keenly scrutinizing the fallen spidren. "Commendable job, lads," he declared.

"We're accustomed to this," replied the Son, his chest puffed out in youthful pride.

"To teamwork?"

"Indeed. The Agents and the Sons. Our numbers alone can't withstand an all-out onslaught. So, we combine our strengths."

"Every one of us brings something unique to the table," the young Agent chimed in, his voice ripe with unwavering self-assuredness. "Agents excel in urban combat, while Sons are adept at high-level martial and arcane arts. Thus, we form a formidable alliance."

Arcane arts, eh? Sven couldn't help but recall Rogerton's abysmal attempt at spellcasting earlier. If the young man was representative of the Sons' magical abilities, it was no wonder they sought external assistance in their conflict against Abaddon.

A rasping voice from behind him sliced through his thoughts. "Shatterfist," it croaked. He whirled around to find the first spidren he had battled. While it lay in a pool of its own greenish lifeblood, twitching in its death throes, it managed to raise its head, eight small eyes fixed on him.

"You know my name?" Sven voiced his suspicion, his eyes narrowed. He wasn't about to let his guard down, especially not within possible striking distance.

Yet, the spidren didn't retaliate. Its labored breathing echoed in the stillness of the night, its voice strained with evident agony.

"All beings in this realm are aware of you, Shatterfist," it wheezed out. "We all know why you're here. Abaddon is aware."

Abaddon knows?

Despite the element of surprise, Sven managed to maintain his composed demeanor. He understood the creature's tactic— unsettling him, forcing him off balance.

"Intriguing," was his curt response.

"I've been eager to meet you since I first heard of you," the spidren continued, its voice barely above a whisper. "You didn't disappoint. There's power within you, Shatterfist, yet not as much as you crave. The rest of your strength is locked away within you. It's there but you can't get to it. Funny, isn't it?

"Not exactly my idea of humor," Sven retorted, a scowl on his face.

A fit of coughing seized the spidren, causing its green lifeblood to splatter the stones beneath it. "Perhaps not from your perspective. But for us, it's an amusing spectacle. A hero summoned, yet shackled by his own summoning."

With those last words, the creature collapsed onto its back, all eight legs pointed towards the heavens in a clear sign of demise.

To make certain, Sven nudged it lightly with his boot. No movement confirmed his suspicion— the beast was indeed deceased.

"We should regroup with the others," he

suggested, his gaze sweeping across the square. "Assess if they need assistance."

His young companions shared an apprehensive glance, their eyes flicking back to the spidren that had just died. As they cleaned their weapons, their wariness was palpable. Deciding to eradicate any lingering doubt, Sven swiftly severed its head.

"An impressive performance," a familiar voice croaked.

He didn't need to turn to identify the speaker. The High Cleric was approaching him, a contorted grimace that could barely pass for a smile etched on his face.

"Appreciate it," Sven responded tersely. The High Cleric was the last person he wished to encounter at this moment.

"Did you enjoy yourself?" the elder asked, an unsettling gleam in his eyes.

Enjoy? He'd just spent exhausting hours in brutal combat to shield the city from an imminent menace. Lives had been lost. Innocence snatched away as children were drafted into the demon's service. His experience was far from enjoyable.

Yet a disturbing question snuck into his mind. *Had he found some twisted pleasure in the mayhem?*

He quickly squashed the disconcerting thought and turned to face the Cleric.

"We prevailed," he said curtly. "That's all that counts."

"Very well," the old man responded, a semblance of satisfaction in his voice. "I have another assignment for you."

Another mission? The High Cleric's nonchalance was alarming. The city had been under a demonic rampage, innocents preyed upon, destruction running wild, and yet the man seemed unfazed. Crossing his arms, Sven gave him the same look he'd given every drunk who tried to make a scene at his grill.

"Have I not been serving your purpose thus far?" Sven questioned. "Engaging these enemies, risking everything?"

"A fresh task, Shatterfist," the cleric clarified, unfazed. "Abaddon's minions will continue to invade as long as their master lives. The true victory lies in his defeat. Battling his lowly followers won't bring us closer to that."

"I see."

The High Cleric furrowed his brow, a sign of deep thought. "There is a dungeon to the south that might hold the key to our success. It's known as the Wailing Chambers. We suspect that a relic of great power resides within, one that might hold a part of the answer we seek. If we can secure enough of these relics, we might just be able to stand against Abaddon."

An exasperated sigh escaped from Sven. He was growing tired of the constant orders, of always being at someone else's beck and call. But the images from his vision wouldn't leave him—the innocent child transformed into a brainless servant, the helpless citizens of Westville living in fear. This was his calling, wasn't it? His purpose. He was born to assist in times of dire need.

"All right," he conceded with a wearied nod. "Give me a steed, a reliable map, and I'll endeavor to achieve what you ask."

The High Cleric revealed a yellowed smile, his decaying teeth in full display. "Excellent. I'll assign Demetrius to accompany you. His knowledge of the terrain should be beneficial. You'll embark at dawn. May fortune be with you."

CHAPTER 17: FORWARD ON ORDERS

The High Cleric's foot was drumming on the cobblestones in a rapid rhythm, signaling his impatience as Sven spoke his goodbyes to the young duo he'd fought alongside, offering them a few helpful pointers. They latched onto his every word, their eyes wide with curiosity and admiration.

"Do you think you'll return?" queried the young Agent, an undertone of hope in his voice. "We could certainly use the additional support."

Sven's gaze strayed towards the Cleric, who responded with a nonchalant shrug.

"Depends on the outcome of future events,"

the Cleric replied, his eyes locked onto Sven. "Now, Shatterfist, it's time we departed."

Noticing Sven's moment of hesitation, the Cleric's glance fell pointedly on the chain dangling from his neck. The silent message was received loud and clear. With the feeling of being trapped in an open-air penitentiary, Sven trailed behind the cleric, making their way back to the fortress of the Sons.

Upon his arrival at the grand doors of the Great Hall, a swarm of youthful faces dashed towards him. However, the High Cleric stepped in, sending them away with a flick of his hand.

"Give him some space," the Cleric commanded. "The man needs rest. Demetrius, step forward."

Demetrius complied, his face ashen, clearly bracing himself for some form of reprimand.

"Your task tomorrow is to guide Shatterfist to the Wailing Chambers, at daybreak. Study your maps tonight, if needed. You'll be provided with two steeds from our stables and ensure you are armed with fresh blades before departure."

He had to force himself not to scowl. Showing that the High Clerics high handed tactics were getting to him would only make the old bag of bones happy. Yet... *how kind of him to provide the necessary tools for a mission he was forced to do.*

However, the cleric's orders were met with sheer elation from Demetrius. "You... you trust me with such an assignment? I—I assure you, Shatterfist, we'll reach our destination. We'll make it as swiftly as possible!"

Sven simply responded with a curt nod, "Good." He had more to say, but the Cleric raised a weathered hand, interrupting him.

"No more discussions," the Cleric declared. "You have an early start. Demetrius, your maps await. Shatterfist, retire to your quarters."

"Wait just a moment," Sven protested, his voice a resonant rumble of defiance. He glared at the Cleric, clenching his fists at his sides. "Who are you to dictate my every move?"

The Cleric merely raised an eyebrow, a slight smirk tugging at the corners of his mouth. "I am merely advising you, Shatterfist."

"Your 'advice' sounds much like an order," Sven replied, his tone sour.

Suddenly, an intense, searing pain radiated from the chain around his neck, causing Sven to stagger. It felt as though a molten whip had been lashed across his throat. As he reached up instinctively to the source of the pain, he could feel the metal links of the chain glowing hot against his skin.

"Remember your place, Shatterfist," the Cleric said, his smirk turning into a full-fledged smile. "You are here for a purpose, and you will fulfill it."

Sven took a deep breath, the searing sensation lessening gradually. He looked up, meeting the cleric's gaze with his own blazing eyes.

"This chain won't safeguard you forever, Cleric," Sven warned, his voice laced with ice. "You might want to remember that."

The High Cleric himself guided Sven to his quarters, and as the door was drawn shut, Sven caught the unmistakable echo of a lock turning. His conditions had transformed from an open-air confinement to a traditional incarceration. The weight of the chain around his neck felt particularly burdensome as he reclined on the bed, eyes closed, attempting to filter out the last rays of sunlight seeping through the grimy windows. He contemplated his predicament, wondering how much longer he would have to endure it. He had to find an escape, regardless of the risk involved.

Slumber came to him eventually, but it was marred by dreams—or were they memories of Ash and Kaleigh.? In it, he was back in the diner, much like the last time they had all been together. However, a tangible melancholy now loomed over the scene, a stark difference from the past. Ash's eyes, reddened from shed tears, reflected deep sorrow. Kaleigh, noticeably lacking her usual vivacity, went about her duties, filling coffee mugs for customers. Once she was done, she sunk onto a stool by the counter.

"Do you think dad will ever return?" she asked, her voice heavy.

Ash's response was distant, as though carried on the wind from afar. "I don't know," she admitted. "I don't know."

Awakening to the faint light of pre-dawn, Sven was left with an unsettled feeling. Was that merely a dream or had he witnessed the reality unfolding on Earth without his presence? The mere thought of Ash and Kaleigh in distress, powerless to change their situation, gnawed at his heart.

I must return home, he resolved. Regardless of the consequences.

His introspection was interrupted by a gentle knock on the door, prompting him to action.

"Wait a moment," he replied, his tone harsher than intended.

"No hurry," came the response in Demetrius'

voice. "Inform me when ready."

Swiftly, Sven dressed and knocked on the door to signal his readiness. The lock was undone, and the door swung open to reveal Demetrius, outfitted for travel and wearing an ear-to-ear grin.

"I've gone through the maps," he announced, gesturing to the satchel slung over his shoulder. "The horses are prepared as well. The High Cleric allowed me to select our mounts, and I picked the fastest ones. If all goes well, we should reach the Wailing Chambers by afternoon."

"Excellent," Sven responded, letting out a deep sigh. Despite the lad's unwavering optimism, Sven wished for a quieter start to the day. Perhaps he could persuade Demetrius to maintain a respectful silence during the initial hours of their expedition. "Very well, let's begin."

Sven had to admit, Demetrius' choice in horses was commendable. Soon enough, he found himself comfortably mounted on a docile, black mare, a brand-new sword securely fastened at his side. As they ventured out of the city and into the boundless fields, the sun began to emerge over the treetops. Leaving Westville in their wake, the day seemed to hold promise—ignoring the impending dungeon raid, of course. With the sun's rays warming his face, Sven found himself absent-mindedly humming a cheerful melody.

However, his companion seemed less than thrilled. "Hold on," Demetrius called, guiding his horse to keep pace with Sven's. "Don't do that."

"Why not?" Sven asked.

"Demons on the road. They'll hear you and attack."

Sven merely shrugged. "And? We can hold our own in a fight. Isn't combating demons the purpose of our journey?"

Demetrius seemed on the verge of responding, but Sven interrupted him by quickening his horse's pace and resuming his melody. If demons were lurking, let them make their move. They would be met with far more resistance than anticipated. Reluctantly, Demetrius followed, maintaining a safe distance between his steed and Sven's.

Sven couldn't help but wonder, *If he's this anxious about potential demons, how will he manage during a dungeon raid?*

His thoughts were abruptly cut short. A group of skeletal Undead burst forth from the nearby bushes, creating a discordant symphony of rattling bones. They stood gazing at the pair, jaws slack, revealing decayed, yellowed teeth. Halting his horse, Sven unsheathed his sword and dismounted.

Ready for the confrontation.

"Time to engage, lad," he called out, glancing over his shoulder. "Prepare yourself."

The jingling of Demetrius' spurs signaled his dismount. Side by side they stood, weapons brandished, a united front against the Undead.

"Follow my lead," Sven said—and then he charged forward, sword already in the air and swinging.

The skeletons moved in, bones chattering, eyes burning with malice, and soon Sven was in the heart of the Undead swarm. He let his body and reflexes take over as he fought, moving with practiced grace and trying to make each strike count. The sound of clashing steel and shattering bone filled the air as he felled one skeleton after another.

When he looked over at Demetrius, though, the lad was still standing frozen, staring at the Undead like a frightened deer.

"Come on!" Sven shouted. "Move!"

Demetrius obeyed, looking like he'd just woken up from a dream. He waded into the fray, blade slashing through the air ferociously. Sven watched him out of the corner of his eye, just in case—but the boy didn't seem to need help. He lacked Sven's finesse but he was doing well enough with what training he had, his youthful strength and sheer force of will.

As the battle raged on, Sven felt himself starting to tire. The Undead were stronger than the demon minions he'd faced the day before, and his old strength still eluded him. He fought back a roar of frustration as a skeleton's steel axe passed within inches of his head—too close. In the old days he would never have let it get that close.

Demetrius came to the rescue. Seeing Sven's fatigue, he stepped forward and felled the axe-wielding skeleton, then pivoted and neatly decapitated another with a single blow.

"You all right?" he said, looking over at Sven.

"Fine. Good work, lad. Keep going."

He nodded and moved back toward the remaining cluster of skeletons. The two fought together, their swords moving as one as they worked to clear the reset of the Undead from the road.

He's good. Really good. Like me when I was that age.

Untrained still, but with strong instincts. The boy could be a great warrior someday if he was lucky and worked hard. Sven wasn't sure if S-Rankers still existed in the world, but if they did Demetrius had the potential to be one.

With each skeleton vanquished, the duo inched closer to victory. They pushed themselves harder as the remaining Undead forces dwindled, their ranks thinning like mist before the morning sun. Finally the last skeletal warrior crumbled to dust beneath Sven's blade.

Demetrius was breathing hard, clearly worn out by the fight—and they had miles of road to cover with a dungeon raid ahead of them.

"Drink," Sven said, cleaning his blade and sheathing it. "Did you pack food?"

"Lots. Dried meat, cheese, bread. Traveler's rations but plenty of them."

"Eat something, then. Get your strength back. And spend more time on the training field, build up your stamina for a fight."

"I've battled before," Demetrius said, a bit defensively. "But not Undead like this. Usually we avoid fighting them when we're out on the road."

"Do you want to clear your world of demons or not?" Sven said, taking a big bite of jerky. "Because if you do you'll have to fight them at some point."

Demetrius took a sip of water from his flask. "Right."

"What's the issue?"

"It's just the High Cleric," the lad said. "He likes things done a specific way. And if he doesn't want us doing something…well, we've no choice but to obey."

Sven frowned. That didn't make sense. Weren't they supposed to be clearing this world of Abaddon's influence? Why wouldn't the Cleric want them to fight off demons? Had he ordered the lads not to fight on the road, or…?

"He saved us, you know," Demetrius said. "From the orphanages and—well, from other places. We owe him. I know it might seem strange to you, but trust that there are reasons for everything I do."

He could tell by the look on the boy's face that he wasn't going to get more of an explanation than that, so he let it go. Instead, he packed up the rest of the meat and mounted up.

"Let's get back on the move," he said. "We'll want to get to the dungeon and make camp before nightfall."

This world was odd and unsettling, with

demons wandering the roads and storming cities. Stranger still was the fact that no one seemed to care, or to think that the current state of affairs was in any way unusual. Maybe they were all so used to it that they'd forgotten that things could be any other way.

They passed through rolling fields and into dense pine forest, and soon they were making their way up a long and rocky incline. Several times they were ambushed by demons, but every time they fought them back. Sven and Demetrius soon found a good rhythm and fought together well, exchanging attacks and covering each other's backs when needed. He could see the boy studying his moves, learning from his fighting style, and several times he used attacks he'd seen Sven use in an earlier skirmish.

The trip took him back to his youth, back when he was still a lowly F-Ranker adventuring around the Kingdom of White Lions with his friends. Those friends had all died or left the life behind over the years, but in their early days they'd all thought they were invincible. He'd made many a dungeon run just like this one, searching for treasure.

Finally, as the afternoon started to shade into

evening, Demetrius held up a hand.

"We should be here. According to my map, the dungeon entrance is within feet of us."

Sven cast a critical eye over their surroundings. To him, it appeared as though they were flanked by nothing more than rocky cliffs and dense foliage.

"Where is it supposed to be?" Sven questioned, the skepticism clear in his voice. He could see no entrance, hidden or otherwise, only a formidable wall of stone.

"I am not entirely sure," Demetrius confessed, his brow creased in a frown. He began to shuffle nervously, "Let me try to—"

"Hold on a moment," Sven interrupted, his attention riveted to an anomaly on the cliff face.

A shadow was cast across the rock, appearing out of place and unnatural. He dismounted his horse, his boots crunching on the gravel as he approached the cliff. Up close, the reason for the misplaced shadow became apparent: a narrow fissure in the rock, almost invisible to an untrained eye, and just wide enough for a man to squeeze through.

"Look here," Sven called out, his voice echoing slightly in the narrow crack, "our entrance to the underground labyrinth."

Returning to his horse, he began the process of unpacking his saddlebags, pulling out their camping gear and food rations.

"Tonight, we rest under the stars. We'll take turns standing guard. When dawn breaks, we make our foray into the unknown," he stated, his eyes fixed on the fissure in the cliff. His mind was already strategizing for the challenges that lay ahead in the belly of the mysterious dungeon.

CHAPTER 18:
DEN GUARDIAN

As the veil of twilight descended, Demetrius began setting up their makeshift camp. He procured two bedrolls from his saddlebags, spreading them out on the soft grass. Meanwhile, Sven attended to their trusty steeds, making sure they were well fed and had a comfortable spot to rest and graze.

"I'll take up the mantle of the first sentinel," Demetrius offered, his voice resolute.

Sven nodded his approval. "Sound decision. Lighting a fire tonight would be unwise—we are within the shadow of the dungeon. It could serve as an invitation for unwanted guests."

"That was the rationale behind my packing. Only dry consumables—jerky, nuts, and the like.

Preparing a meal without the option of fire would be...challenging."

Sven raised an eyebrow, impressed. "An admirable bit of forethought there, lad."

As he unpacked their frugal dinner, a bold thought blazed in his mind. What if he could somehow transport Ash and Kaleigh to this world? He could take Demetrius and some of the other lads on quests, train them, improve his own skills, perhaps even impart some adventuring wisdom to Kaleigh when she was ready.

But a shadow of reality quickly doused the flame of his idea. Ash was not as he was now —young, full of vigor. The likelihood of her undergoing the same rejuvenation he experienced was uncertain. He could not, in good conscience, force her into a world where she might be trapped in an aging body while he appeared to have bathed in the mythical fountain of youth. It was an unfair proposition.

However, a man was allowed his flights of fancy.

They consumed their meal in relative silence. Sven settled down for his brief rest while Demetrius assumed his post as guard. Slumber crept up on him like a stealthy rogue, and before he knew it, he was awakened to take his turn.

"Everything is under control," Demetrius reassured him quickly, a tired yawn escaping his lips. "It's your watch now. Gods, I need to rest."

Sven nodded, understanding the lad's fatigue. They had journeyed far from Westville, and the multiple skirmishes along the way had taken a toll. "Rest well, Demetrius. I'll be alert, and I'll rouse you at dawn. Should any mishap occur, you'll be the first to know."

The serenity of the night allowed Sven to ruminate in peace. He kept a vigilant watch, but the area remained tranquil, devoid of any monstrous intrusion. A suspicious tranquility, considering the demon-infested road they had traversed. Were the beasts resting, or was there something so ominous within the dungeon that it held them at bay? They could only confirm upon venturing into the abyss.

Demetrius stirred from his sleep just as the first light of dawn started to kiss the sky. Together, they took care of their horses, ensuring they were watered and securely fastened.

"I've packed torches," Demetrius informed Sven, pulling out a bunch of them, their ends soaked in oil for long-lasting light.

"Spare ones?"

"Abundant," the lad assured him.

Sven sparked a flame to life on one of the torches. They advanced towards the dungeon, the chilling narrow entrance forcing them to enter single file—a rather inauspicious beginning.

"We proceed swiftly but tread cautiously," he directed. "Our priority is to locate a spacious passage, allowing us to stand together. Are you prepared, lad?"

"I...I believe so," Demetrius replied, a hint of trepidation in his voice.

"Then it's time. Onward."

Sven led the charge, stepping into the intimidating labyrinth. The passage turned abruptly, and they found themselves embraced by an inky blackness, the flickering torch their only source of illumination.

"Do you have any knowledge about this dungeon, lad?" Sven asked, his voice bouncing off the narrow stone walls.

"All I know is what the High Cleric relayed to me," Demetrius replied. "It's an ancient structure, shrouded in mystery, feared and avoided by all. An old tale talks of thieves who pilfered a relic from the Clerisy and sought refuge in this very dungeon. They vanished, never to be seen again. But who can say how much of that is truth and how much is myth?"

A wry smile crept onto Sven's face. "Let me hazard a guess. The relic we are here to retrieve...it's the same one, isn't it?"

"Could there be more than one?" Demetrius responded, uncertainty lacing his voice.

As they advanced further, the narrow entrance opened up into a slightly more accommodating passageway. While still constricted, it allowed them to stand side by side, a somewhat comforting prospect. After wiggling his way into the dungeon, Sven found his muscles tense. He took a moment, indulging in a full-body stretch, appreciating the smaller, agile body he now inhabited.

As he scanned their surroundings, it was clear that this hallway had been the result of human craftsmanship. The evidence lay in the metal brackets affixed to the stone walls, once housing flaming torches, now only empty holders. He positioned the torch he was carrying into one of these brackets, using the free hands to unpack and ignite another one.

"Demetrius, do you carry chalk with you?" he

asked, his gaze still sweeping the surroundings.

"What color?" Demetrius inquired.

Suppressing a chuckle, Sven replied, "The hue doesn't matter. We'll be using it for marking our path on these stone walls, to find our way back when necessary. Choose a color that stands out."

Obediently, Demetrius produced a bright yellow chalk stick. With it, Sven etched a prominent X beside the dungeon's entrance, then reclaimed the torch from its bracket. Leading the way, they delved deeper into the dungeon. The temperature dropped gradually, while the sound of water dripping resonated ominously around them. The moist chill of the air was palpable, indicating a descent deeper into the underground dungeon.

Their journey within the dungeon took a perilous turn when the floor beneath them transformed from stone to dirt. With a sudden burst of movement, the ground came alive, and gigantic serpents emerged from their burrows, brandishing long, venomous fangs. Sven reacted instantly, his sword swinging down with full force, only to ricochet off the tough scales of the serpents. The constricting passageway denied him the room for a more effective swing.

To his astonishment, Demetrius reacted with impressive bravery. The young lad drew a pair of daggers from his bag, swiftly evading the lunging jaws of the serpents as he darted around looking for openings to strike. His blades whistled through the air, landing shallow strikes on the serpent bodies. But for each snake he managed to injure, two more retaliated. His attacks, while brave, barely impeded the onslaught of the creatures.

"We need to join forces, lad!" Sven roared above the hissing serpents.

With a resolute stride, he plunged himself into the swarm of serpents, instantly drawing their attention towards him. While his sword still failed to penetrate their armored scales, he successfully diverted their focus from Demetrius. His only hope lay in the lad seizing this opportunity. Despite his newfound youth, his strength had its limits, and the horde of serpents was incessantly testing those limits. He could only pray that Demetrius would act swiftly.

With the serpents' attention squarely on Sven, Demetrius seized the opportunity and sprang into action. Utilizing his nimble agility, he danced around the serpents, wielding his twin daggers with deadly precision. Each swift thrust was followed by a rapid retreat, ensuring he remained unscathed. Sven, on the other hand, adopted a more defensive strategy. His sword intercepted any offensive maneuvers aimed at Demetrius, creating a protective barrier around the young lad.

Together, they operated like a well-oiled machine. Their synergy and unyielding determination gradually began to deplete the serpent ranks. Each successful strike from Demetrius brought down a serpent, boosting his confidence and resolve. On the other hand, Sven held his ground, using his superior strength and experience to keep the serpents' focus on him and providing Demetrius with ample opportunity to strike.

After what seemed like an eternity, the final snake fell, defeated and lifeless, littering the passageway with remnants of the fierce battle. Panting heavily, Demetrius looked around, visibly in awe of their victory.

"That was an impressive display, lad," Sven praised, patting him roughly on the back. "How does victory taste?"

"My first dungeon..." Demetrius started, cleaning off his daggers on the side of his pants. He looked around at the dead serpents, then a smile crept on his face. "It was...incredible?"

"Indeed, it was," Sven agreed, reminiscing about his first dungeon experience. Just like Demetrius, he had been eager and excited for the fight, the thrill of exploration. It was a sensation that took him back to his earlier days.

"Should we continue?" Demetrius asked, regaining his breath.

"More challenges lie ahead," Sven responded. "From my experience, the enemies get stronger the further we delve."

"Excellent," Demetrius replied, determination gleaming in his eyes.

Sharing a hearty laugh, they pressed on, holding their torches high. The synergy between them made Sven nostalgic, reminding him of his days as a young adventurer in the Kingdom of White Lions and the comrades he made during that time. The thrill of exploration and combat made him feel truly rejuvenated, a stark contrast to his previous life as a diner cook.

A part of him had chosen the tranquil life; he remembered how weary he had felt towards the end of his tenure in the Kingdom. He had been ready to retire, to live out his days in obscurity.

The prospect of cooking burgers and brewing coffee instead of saving the world had brought him immense satisfaction. But now, in this new era, he found himself questioning his past choices. The monotony of his past life seemed rather dull in contrast to the adrenaline-filled life of a dungeon explorer.

Noticing his quiet contemplation, Demetrius inquired, "Everything okay?"

"Just reminiscing. Let's keep moving."

Despite Demetrius' skeptical gaze, they continued their journey deeper into the dungeon. Sven held his sword at the ready, prepared for any challenge that lay ahead. His years of dungeon exploring had ingrained in him the anticipation of the upcoming battles, and he welcomed them wholeheartedly.

Sure enough, as they turned the next corner, they saw it: a colossal serpent coiled in a slightly wider passageway than the one they were in. Its body seemed to stretch endlessly into the dungeon, and its fangs dripped venom. Its menacing presence was enhanced by the fact that it was encircled by a writhing mass of tiny, poisonous snakes.

"That's a lot of snakes," Demetrius said,

looking disgusted.

"Sure is."

Sven drew his sword. The sooner they could get through this, the better.

The large snake saw them and hissed—and the two adventurers exchanged a silent nod. Time to go

They charged forward together, blades out and striking. Demetrius was faster—and the first to get to the mother snake. He danced around the giant serpent's lunges, his agile movements evading its fangs. With each swing, his blade found its mark, and the large snake snarled its fury. The tiny snakes responded to their mother's distress, lunging at Demetrius' legs and wrapping themselves around him so he couldn't move.

Sven sprang into action. He slashed at the tiny snakes with his broadsword, freeing the lad so he could keep attacking the mother serpent. Then *he* went on the offensive, striking with his blade, mowing down little snakes as he went. They needed to clear out the passage so the large snake was the only one left—otherwise the children would keep trying to stop them. Demetrius realized what he was doing and joined in, neatly sidestepping the large snake's fangs every time she tried to attack.

The battle raged on, the air full of hissing and the sickening sound of metal on scales and bone. Sven and Demetrius worked together well, each anticipating the other's needs and providing the necessary support. Finally, when about half the little snakes were dead, Sven held up a hand.

"I'll go in," he said. "You keep at it."

Demetrius, with a nod of acknowledgment, continued his relentless onslaught against the numerous smaller serpents. His blades danced in the dim torchlight, slashing and hacking at the writhing mass of snakes. Simultaneously, he shielded Sven from their intrusive intervention, ensuring that the veteran adventurer was free to tackle their massive adversary.

Sven, for his part, met the daunting challenge head-on. His strikes landed with calculated precision on the colossal serpent, each blow a testament to his S-Ranker prowess. Evading the snake's venomous fangs and flailing tail, Sven continued his assault. Gradually, the mother snake's strength started to ebb, her retaliation slowing under the weight of his incessant strikes.

Sven's muscles screamed in protest, the fatigue of the prolonged battle taking its toll.

But he refused to yield, the relic's potential value propelling him forward.

Summoning a final surge of energy, Sven executed a decisive strike, his blade plunging deep into the snake's heart. The dungeon echoed with the serpent's agonizing roar as it writhed in its death throes. As its enormous tail thrashed wildly, Sven deftly avoided the desperate final strike and watched as the monstrosity slowly succumbed.

To ensure its demise, Sven dealt a final blow, but it went unacknowledged. The gigantic serpent lay still, its reign of terror finally ended.

Reacting to the fall of their guardian, the remaining smaller snakes attempted to scatter, seeking refuge in the confines of the dungeon. But Sven and Demetrius quickly engaged in a mop-up operation. With precise strikes, they prevented any snake from escaping, ensuring that no remnant of this serpent brood would grow into a future menace.

With the elimination of the final snake, a momentary calm descended upon them. However, this was abruptly shattered as the ground beneath them quaked violently. Sven, momentarily thrown off balance, grasped the wall for support.

A sense of foreboding washed over him.

Something ominous was approaching.

CHAPTER 19: COMRADE

As quickly as the ominous rumbling had arisen, it receded, leaving the pair of warriors standing amidst a sea of snake corpses. The silence weighed heavy upon the air.

"What just happened?" Demetrius queried, his voice tinged with a note of fear.

While Sven was casually wiping his blade clean, his instincts were anything but relaxed. He kept his senses on high alert, his veteran instincts telling him they were far from safe. "We haven't met the boss of the dungeon. It's most likely lurking deeper within," Sven informed the younger adventurer, his tone cool and steady. "And it's massive. My gut tells me we'll be clashing with it sooner rather than later."

"But... wasn't the giant serpent supposed to be the final boss?" Demetrius asked, doubt clouding his eyes.

Sven merely shook his head, a hint of a smile on his lips. "Where's the relic then, lad?"

Without needing to verbalize his response, Demetrius's grim silence spoke volumes. He hefted his satchel higher, steeling himself as he trailed behind Sven, venturing deeper into the serpent-infested dungeon.

As they carefully navigated around the sea of deceased snakes and through a distant door, the flickering light from their torches abruptly extinguished, plunging them into pitch-black darkness. A palpable sense of unease settled in the room as Demetrius hastily rummaged through his pack.

"Hurry, lad," Sven urged, a silent prayer for safety echoing in his mind. "We don't want to be blind for too long."

Almost as if his words had stirred the beast, the ground beneath them quaked once more. The ominous rumbling resonated from the depths, signaling the turning of something massive.

"Here."

With the ignition of fresh torches, Demetrius

swiftly ended their time in darkness. The pair stood, torches held aloft, their glances darting around to reassure themselves. However, their immediate surroundings held nothing but emptiness.

"Whatever it is, it's further down the path," Sven advised, his voice barely above a whisper. "Let's tread carefully, lad. This relic needs to justify this risk."

"As the High Cleric commands, so it shall be," Demetrius stated, his belief unwavering.

Sven rolled his eyes in response, making sure to turn away so Demetrius couldn't catch his action. How he wished the Sons would abandon their blind faith in that eerie old man.

As they silently trudged down the subsequent passageway, their senses remained sharp for any potential threats. The environment became increasingly cold and damp, a telltale sign of descending deeper into the earth. The floor sloped downwards, and the sounds of unseen movement from ahead became more frequent and discernible.

"By the gods, we must be deep underground by now," Demetrius uttered, his voice echoing off the rocky walls.

A sense of disquiet coursed through Sven at his words. The thought of being so deep beneath the earth, with no immediate means of escape, always unnerved him. The impending doom of being trapped under tons of rock if the earth decided to crumble…he preferred his battles on open ground, under the boundless sky. But here, in the crushing depths of a dungeon, all options seemed scarce.

"Aye," Sven responded curtly to Demetrius, his mind buried deep in contemplation. The lad was wound up enough as it was; he didn't need the raw fears of a veteran adventurer adding to his stress. "But our journey's end is nearing, lad. I believe we have only a short distance left to tread."

"Until we confront…whatever beast awaits us," Demetrius chimed in, his tone betraying his mounting anxiety.

"Exactly. Remain vigilant and keep your blade at the ready," Sven advised, maintaining a cool exterior despite the rising tension. "Your deftness with the daggers earlier was commendable. A repeat performance might come in handy."

A bone-chilling shriek echoed from the heart of the labyrinth, abruptly severing their exchange. The creature, it seemed, was alarmingly close now.

"I believe our adversary is just around the next

bend," Sven whispered, his voice barely audible. "Easy does it, lad."

His prediction was vindicated as they cautiously navigated the next narrow, serpentine passageway, only to stumble upon a cavernous chamber. Like the rest of the dungeon, metal brackets designed to hold torches lined the walls, yet here they were not bare. Alien, green flames flickered from reed torches, casting an unsettling illumination on the cavernous surroundings.

A colossal hydra, significantly larger than the one Sven had previously bested, resided in the chamber's heart. Its many heads twisted and undulated, each one sporting a jaw lined with formidable fangs. Upon hearing the intruders, the creature's multiple heads swiveled in their direction.

"So," the creature's voice reverberated through the chamber. "You have finally arrived. From the very beginning, I sensed your presence, heard the cries of my progeny as you mercilessly slaughtered them. I anticipated your arrival, aware of your intent to challenge me."

"Correct," Sven replied nonchalantly, his demeanor unyielding. "You read us well."

As he uttered these words, his gaze swept the

area behind the hydra, searching...until it fell on the wall opposite. A pulsating blue orb, secured firmly to the wall, caught his eye.

That has to be the relic.

This realization cemented his understanding that they were at the final stage of the dungeon. They had to endure this one last ordeal, and then freedom would be theirs. A daunting task lay ahead, especially considering the already exhausting journey and multiple combats that had preceded it. Demetrius was clearly inexperienced in confronting hydras, his attempt to maintain a facade of courage doing little to veil his underlying fear. Sven had been around fledgling adventurers long enough to discern pretense from true bravery.

"Hold your nerve, lad. This is the moment." Sven cautioned.

"You will not kill me," the hydra continued, its tone seething with contempt. "I will be the one to claim your lives, and once I have, I will revel in devouring your flesh and crunching your bones, much like I did with those who dared challenge me before."

Sven rolled his eyes at the hydra's monologue. It seemed every dungeon boss had an identical script. Threatening to the uninitiated, perhaps, but to a veteran like him, it was tiresome.

"Bold words," Sven interrupted, his voice laced with a trace of boredom. "But I've heard them all before. You wouldn't believe how many of your brethren have spouted the same script. Rather lacking in originality, aren't we?"

The hydra recoiled slightly, an unnerving hiss escaping from each of its many throats. "You dare to mock me? You, an insignificant human?!"

Sven shrugged nonchalantly. "Well, yes. You see, you're not the first hydra I've crossed paths with. In fact," he continued, a sly smile playing at the corner of his mouth, "I've killed so many of your kind that I've lost count. Killing hydras is sort of my specialty, you could say."

The hydra's heads swayed angrily, its eyes glowing ominously in the dim light. "You lie! You wish to intimidate me with your empty boasts!"

"Believe what you will," Sven retorted, his tone unflappable. "But the fact remains that I've faced enough hydras to practically be on a first-name basis. I've spent some much time around Hydra's, one in particular we could have practically clinked steins together in a tavern, had circumstances been different, and the Hydra had hands."

The cavern echoed with the hydra's enraged hisses, its many heads weaving restlessly. Sven's blasé attitude seemed to have struck a nerve, and its anger was palpable.

Sven turned his head towards Demetrius, his voice dropping to a low whisper. "Things are about to get heated."

Sven, moving with the fluid grace of a seasoned fighter, lunged and weaved as the hydra's heads struck out, anticipating each move with deadly precision. His blade met scales and flesh with a satisfying crunch, severing one head after another.

His voice echoed within the cavern's vast expanse, smooth as silk yet sharp as the blade he wielded, "Demetrius, now!"

As if a string puppet adhering to the whims of its master, Demetrius sprang into action, brandishing the torch with newfound resolve. Each stump left by Sven's sword was quickly met with flames that danced violently, hungry to consume. They singed the hydra's flesh, stemming the regrowth and eliciting a tortured roar from the beast.

In between his precise maneuvers, Sven glanced back at the boy, his gaze approving. "Well done, lad. You're getting the hang of it."

Demetrius offered a nod, his face flushed with the thrill of combat and perhaps, a sense of accomplishment. "I'm learning from the best."

Sven turned back to face their monstrous adversary, a smirk tugging at the corner of his lips. "Hear that, Hydra? You're not even an adequate teacher. They all want to learn from me."

Despite the predicament they were in, the camaraderie between the pair sparked a flicker of levity, their exchanged words of mockery to the hydra echoed in the cavernous chamber, each syllable carrying a defiant challenge.

Th hydra, however, was far from amused. A guttural growl erupted from the depths of its many throats. "Do you think your insignificant flames can stop me? I am the terror of the underworld!"

Sven rolled his eyes at the creature's theatrics, the theatrics of a cornered beast. "All talk, no show, Hydra. That's what you are."

He charged forward again, blade and determination shining in tandem, Demetrius right on his heels, torch held high. They were a well-coordinated duo, mainly due to Sven's experience and leadership, and the young boy's eagerness to learn and adapt. The battle was far from over, but they were undeterred, focused solely on their objective.

They were there to retrieve the relic, and no hydra, big or small, was going to stop them.

Demetrius, for his part, nodded and tightened his grip on his weapon, his eyes wide with apprehension and determination. He wasn't a veteran like Sven, but he was learning fast—he had to. They were, after all, in the heart of the beast's den.

Sven's commands echoed in the cavern, his voice sharp and unyielding over the roars of the hydra. "Strike with accuracy! Keep that flame alive, Demetrius! Apply the fire directly to the wound and move swiftly!"

As the heads of the monster fell, its desperation was palpable in its snarls, its frenzied movements, and its attacks that became increasingly fierce. The lad and Sven found themselves on their toes, narrowly evading the venomous snap of the hydra's jaws time and time again.

Yet, Sven kept a clear mind amidst the chaos. He inwardly noted their progress against the monstrosity. Eight heads severed, three remained.

The additional one was a result of his attempt to show Demetrius the danger of not cauterizing.

Did he regret making the battle tougher? Sven dismissed the thought. The lad needed the lesson. He needed to understand the consequences of his actions.

In the whirlwind of battle, the two were unified like a well-oiled machine, the experienced hand of Sven and the enthusiastic young Demetrius moving together in a rhythm borne out of desperate survival. However, the monstrous hydra, once dismissive of them, now recognized the real threat they posed. Its laughter had faded, replaced by the pure instinct to survive as it thrashed and hissed in a futile attempt to reclaim the upper hand.

Just as victory seemed to be within their grasp, disaster ensued. The hydra's tail, a weapon in its own right, lashed out with a force that sent Demetrius sprawling, the boy caught off guard. The ground greeted him harshly, a low groan slipping from his lips as he squirmed under the hydra's tail, the torch thrown aside in the chaos.

Sven's heart pounded in his chest, his mind screaming in alarm. One of the remaining heads had spotted the defenseless lad, its fangs gleaming with anticipation of an easy kill.

Acting on pure instinct, Sven shouted, "Torch!" His command was met by the prompt throw from Demetrius, the boy's terrified eyes watching him as the torch spun in the air towards Sven.

In a fluid motion, Sven severed another head, his sword and torch working in perfect harmony to finish the job. With an unceremonious slash, he managed to free Demetrius from the painful grip of the hydra's tail, the tail recoiling from the sharp sting of his blade.

"Thanks," Demetrius panted, rolling away to a safer distance. His voice was shaky but held a newfound respect for the seasoned adventurer.

Sven simply nodded, words as curt as before, "Don't mention it. Just be more careful next time. I won't always be there to bail you out."

Although exhaustion was beginning to take its toll on both, the sight of the battered hydra, its heads now dragging on the ground, provided a surge of adrenaline. The end was near. They just had to push through, to muster every ounce of energy for one last decisive charge. Sven and Demetrius regrouped, their resolve reignited, and they once again charged at the waning beast.

Their blades sliced through the air, their

movements guided by a will to survive and claim victory over the monstrosity before them.

With each falling head, the once mighty hydra was reduced to a lifeless heap. The last head hit the ground with a resounding thud, and Sven's sword swung down to lop it off while Demetrius, the flame in his hand, seared the wound. The air was thick with the stench of dark ichor and burnt flesh, but it marked the end of the battle. The colossal beast lay defeated, a testament to their hard-won victory.

Sven cautiously approached the relic mounted on the far wall, each step squelching in the gore-soaked ground. His gaze fell on the sticky substance splattered on his boots and he sighed inwardly. "Well, at least they belong to the Sons," he muttered to himself. "They can worry about getting new ones."

The relic was secured tightly to the wall. However, with a tug, Sven easily ripped it off, his heart pounding as a wave of energy washed over him. A rush of knowledge hit him next and he began drowning within its depth.

With every bit of new information, he felt his

strength pulsating, as if he was being replenished from within. This was a familiar sensation, one he had experienced before. He was regaining his lost power, piece by piece.

As the flood of power and knowledge receded, Sven found himself still standing in the same underground cavern. In his grasp, a sword shimmered, its pale purple glow reflecting the flickering torchlight. Its razor-sharp edge gleamed with promise. He looked over to see Demetrius, a pair of new daggers and a sword at his side, an expression of awe etched on his young face.

The adrenaline from the battle was still coursing through Sven's veins, a fiery reminder of why he loved this life—the thrill of the hunt, the camaraderie born out of shared danger, the sense of satisfaction in being the victor. The lad, Demetrius, he was becoming a solid partner, more than Sven initially gave him credit for. He saw a bit of his younger self in him—brash, eager, reckless, but full of potential. The bond between them was reminiscent of the old days, fighting alongside his brothers-in-arms.

Yet, the harsh truth of his current reality couldn't be ignored. The relic was now safely stored away in his satchel, the echo of the High

Cleric's instructions reverberating in his head. As soon as they stepped out of this dungeon, they'd be marching back to the Sons' tower, their temporary sanctuary that felt more like a prison. Once again, he'd be relegated to a pawn in the hands of the old man until another task was deemed fit for him.

Exhaustion was gnawing at his bones, but the thought of going back, of wearing those chains again, sparked a fresh surge of energy. He yearned for another monster, another challenge, just a little more time before he would have to submit to the confines of the tower.

Nevertheless, the charade had to continue for now. With a forced grin, he turned to Demetrius, "Well, lad, we did it. Time to climb out of this dark hole and embrace the sun." The satisfaction in his voice was genuine; the cheerfulness, however, was a mask.

As they prepared to exit, a determined glint hardened in Sven's eyes. It was time to devise a plan. The constraints of the Sons, their summons, it couldn't bind him forever. He had to find a way out. And that way out... needed to be discovered as soon as possible.

CHAPTER 20: TOWARDS FORGIVENESS

The journey back to the surface had Demetrius practically beaming, his mind still reeling from the influx of power granted by the relic. Their path was strewn with lifeless snake bodies, the aftermath of their victorious battle.

Sven, once again, found his boots marred by the dark, viscous ichor. *Just my luck*, he thought, promising himself to demand an upgrade in footwear from the High Cleric upon their return. Boots with a sturdier tread and a thicker sole would surely be suitable compensation for his services. His newly acquired sword felt pleasantly substantial in his grip, though its bestowed name

'Magekiller' was something less than favorable.

Ash, after all, had been a mage. An idea struck him. He turned to his companion, "What, in your opinion, is a fitting name for a sword, lad?"

"Huh?" came the perplexed reply.

"A name, Demetrius. For a sword. Focus."

"Uh...I...don't really know," was the hesitant response.

"Hmm." A mental note was made to devote some serious contemplation to the matter. After all, the name of one's sword held significance. As daylight dwindled, they hastened their pace, yearning to feel the warm embrace of the sun before it disappeared behind the trees. With the hydra no longer a threat, their ascent was met with no resistance.

Before long, they were squeezing through the narrow entrance, emerging victorious. Sven allowed a content smile as the sun's rays touched his face. "Quite an invigorating sensation, isn't it, lad?" he chuckled, "Emerging from a dungeon with treasure in tow." Suddenly, an unfamiliar voice boomed, "HEY!" Instinctually, Sven had his sword drawn, pinning the intruder against the wall, his blade pressed threateningly against the man's throat.

Recognition dawned upon him, "Rogerton?" he questioned, "What in blazes are you doing here?" The young mage stuttered, flustered, "I...I knew you were in the dungeon, and thought...maybe...you might need some...help." Sven retracted, his sword still unsheathed, his arms folded across his chest. His lips curled into a sarcastic grin. "A bit late, wouldn't you agree? And just so we're clear, we managed quite fine without your *help*. Demetrius," he motioned towards the youth, "has proven to be a capable warrior."

Pride swelled within Demetrius at the unexpected compliment, while Rogerton seemed to shrink under Sven's scorn. "Well," he began, faltering over his words, "that's...good. I mean—"

"No, Rogerton," Sven interjected, his tone unyielding, "I'm not in the mood for pleasantries or half-hearted attempts at praise. We've slayed monsters today, defended ourselves against threats you can't even begin to comprehend. So tell me, what's your real motive for being here? You proved quite the disappointment in Westville, your control over your magic lacking at best. Innocent people were put at risk due to your reckless casting during the demon attack. If you can't handle the responsibility, you have no right to wield such power. Don't think I've forgotten the civilians you disregarded so callously. You've got a long way to go before you could be considered a competent mage. So, unless you're here to tell me you've learned some control and respect for others' safety, I suggest you turn around and leave."

Rogerton's face paled significantly at Sven's words, his knees shaking, but he managed to stay upright. Sven leaned in, his voice dropping low and threatening, "And let me make one thing very clear. If I ever hear about you endangering innocent lives again due to your recklessness...I promise you, you'll be eating dirt faster than you can cast a spell. Understand?" Rogerton gulped, nodding weakly, his eyes wide with shock and fear...yet Sven saw a driving will, a passion in the lads eyes. The boy opened his mouth.

"Listen," Sven interrupted, "I've had a long, tiring day. We've slain countless monsters, and I am in no mood for pretending I can tolerate you. We can manage perfectly well on our own, thank you."

Rogerton blanched at Sven's blunt assertion but managed to maintain his stance. Sven raised an eyebrow as the lad stammered out an apology. "I-I know I didn't present myself well before," Rogerton confessed, shifting uncomfortably. "And, well, my battle magic—it wasn't as controlled as I'd have liked. But I promise, I'm working on it. I'm striving to become stronger, more precise. I really am trying." A heavy sigh escaped Sven's lips. These starry-eyed, green adventurers always seemed to gravitate towards him like moths to a flame.

"Listen, Rogerton," Sven began, leaning against the cold stone wall. His voice was firm, yet not unkind, "Magic is not the only path to power. You're better with a blade than you are with a spell. If you hone your skill with different weapons, train relentlessly, you could become a competent warrior. There's honor in that path, too." Perhaps this was why these fledgling adventurers sought him out. Despite his gruff exterior, Sven had a reputation for sharing sage advice. He was a seasoned warrior, after all, a beacon of knowledge in the vast sea of uncertainty that was the adventuring life...or he had been in his previous time line. Sven's blunt critique of Rogerton's magical prowess didn't seem to daunt the young mage. His eyes flickered with a spark of excitement.

"I see, swordsmanship," Rogerton affirmed,

nodding to himself. "If I focus on that, can I...can I join you?"

Sven sighed, pinching the bridge of his nose. "Work on your attitude, too, Rogerton," he admonished. "Westville was no proud moment. A true adventurer puts the safety of innocents above all else. Remember that."

Nodding again, Rogerton repeated Sven's advice to himself. "Attitude. Innocent lives. I'll keep that in mind."

The sun was now merely a faint blush on the horizon. Sven was weary and his stomach grumbled with hunger. His tolerance for life lessons was waning. He yearned for a simple meal, even if it was just travel rations, and a solid night's sleep.

"Stay with us for the night," Sven told Rogerton, waving towards their camp. "See to the horses, make sure they're fed and watered. That'll give Demetrius and me some time to rest. We can discuss your potential future tomorrow."

Rogerton nodded, hurrying off to complete his assigned tasks. Sven gratefully shed his armor, dousing his torch before settling onto the cool earth. He watched as Demetrius began to prepare their food, a contented sigh escaping Sven's lips.

Apprentices made life easier. Back in his younger days, he'd have had to manage everything himself. Now, with the work divided, he had a moment to ponder on a suitable name for his new sword. *Nightsbane? Eclipse? Stormbreaker?* None of the options felt quite right. Before he knew it, the two young men were gathered around him, gnawing on dried jerky and looking at him expectantly. He glanced at them, raising an eyebrow. "What's on your minds?" he asked.

"Do you have any tales from your past adventures?" Demetrius asked, his eyes bright with curiosity. "Something to help pass the time?"

Nibbling on a piece of cheese, Sven nodded. "Sure, I could spin a yarn or two," he conceded, his gaze sweeping between Rogerton and Demetrius. "But in return, I want to hear about how you two got tangled up with the Sons. Is it a deal?"

The lads exchanged a glance before grinning back at Sven, "Deal."

The flickering firelight cast dancing shadows on Rogerton's face, highlighting the uncertain creases on his forehead. He glanced at Sven, his eyes seeming to hold an unspoken question. After a few moments of silence, he finally found his voice. "Sven," he started, his voice shaky, "about what happened in Westville... I wanted to say—I'm sorry. I wasn't in control. People were hurt because of me." Sven watched the young mage closely. His apology seemed sincere. Despite his rash actions, Rogerton appeared to understand the severity of his mistakes.

"I want to learn, Sven. Truly, I do," Rogerton confessed, his gaze lowering to his hands. "Could you... Would you consider teaching me?"

The quiet plea hung in the air, leaving a trail of vulnerability. Sven appraised Rogerton with a scrutinizing gaze. It was one thing to apologize and another to learn from one's mistakes. The path of an adventurer was a treacherous one, and many were the pitfalls that awaited the ill-prepared.

After a drawn-out silence, Sven finally responded. "Alright, lad. You've owned up to your errors, that's the first step. But words are hollow without actions to back them up. If you're sincere, show it in your actions. Learn from your past, be vigilant in the present, and strive for a better future. If you can do that, then yes, I'll consider teaching you."

Rogerton's face lit up with a glimmer of hope, and Sven couldn't help but feel a pang of sympathy for the lad. The road to redemption was a long one, but everyone deserved a chance to walk it. And who knows? Maybe under Sven's watchful eye, Rogerton might even grow into the adventurer he aspired to be and not whatever the High Cleric had molded him to be.

Rogerton, gathering his thoughts, began to share his past. "My story isn't unique among us. Orphaned at three, due to the White Plague. Westville was hit hard, and I think it was the work of the demons. Nothing is certain, though. My parents were taken by the plague, leaving me alone," he paused, swallowing hard. "I had relatives, but they had a farm and thought me useless at that age. Just another mouth to feed without any immediate value for labor. I wasn't aware of it then, but it all became clear later. All I understood at that age was being thrown into an orphanage, expected to clean until my hands were raw, surviving on a diet of bland gruel and hard bread."

Sven listened, his expression softening. The harsh reality of Rogerton's past added depth to his character. It didn't pardon his reckless actions, but it provided context. With a slight nod, he encouraged Rogerton to carry on.

"My days in the orphanage stretched into years," Rogerton continued. "At six, I was sent to work for a baker. The orphanage children were distributed around the town, performing menial tasks far too strenuous for our age. I loathed the heat of the bakery, the constant hauling of heavy sacks of flour. The baker wasn't unkind, but he was indifferent. After all, I wasn't his apprentice. I was merely an extra hand he 'hired' from the orphanage. My nights were spent on freezing stone floors, my diet remained unchanged, and my skinny, underfed frame bore the brunt of all the physical exertion."

Sven turned to Demetrius, who was listening attentively. Demetrius spoke up, "My story aligns closely with yours, Rog. Except my father was a soldier who passed away before I was born. My mother died when I was a little older than you were when you lost yours. She worked in a factory and was involved in some accident. I was never told the details. All I knew was, she was no longer with me." He stared into the fire, memories flickering in his eyes. "With no other family, the orphanage was my only refuge. And we all know what fate has in store for orphans."

"Yeah, we lost track of most of the kids from

the orphanage. Heard later that some died, some ended up behind bars. The place didn't exactly prime us for a bright future," Rogerton added, a somber note coloring his voice. As their stories entwined in the flickering firelight, Sven could see a bond forming between them, one of a shared past. They were not just fellow adventurers; they were companions, sharing their burdens and dreams under the stars.

"So what was your ticket out?" Sven inquired, aiming for casual curiosity despite how much he desired to know this answer. The sad reality was, every world had its own share of oppressive systems. Exploitative individuals, always found ways to take advantage of the helpless. The variation lay only in the methods.

Demetrius, with his gaze fixed upon the drifting clouds, responded, "The High Cleric." His voice held a note of reverence. "One day, he graced the orphanage with his presence. We were prepped for a VIP but kept in the dark about his identity. All of us boys had to get into our best clothes and line up in the main hall. And then, he walked along that line, scrutinizing each one of us. Some he dismissed without a word, to some he offered a few remarks. But for a select few—the fortunate ones—he signaled approval to the headmaster and just like that, we were in his care."

Rogerton nodded in agreement, "Our stories echo. The High Cleric. The lineup." He scratched the back of his neck before he continued, "The suspense of the first choice triggered a frenzy of conjectures. But there was no discernible pattern. The selection seemed utterly arbitrary."

Acknowledging Rogerton's observation, Demetrius added, "Indeed, you would expect him to opt for the robust or the brainy. And sometimes, he did. But the pattern was elusive. To this day, the reason he picked me remains an enigma."

"Same here," Rogerton affirmed. "But, I'm eternally grateful for it. It was a turning point in my life. For the first time, I was not starved or overworked. I had a comfortable bed to rest in, free from the oppressive heat of the bakery. For the initial few months, we were allowed to indulge in leisure—eat, sleep, frolic around the courtyard. We even had access to the Great Hall during colder months. It was a time of unadulterated joy for all the boys. Gradually, we regained our health, adding some much-needed weight."

As Sven listened, he found himself wondering about the peculiar motives of the High Cleric. The whole scenario seemed bizarre, even by the Sons' standards. He posed his question, "Have you ever considered why he chose you?"

"Frankly, no idea," Demetrius confessed. "Among the boys in the orphanage, I was not the fastest, the strongest, or the smartest. Yet, I was chosen, and they were not. Over the years, I have often reflected on this apparent injustice. Why was I liberated while they continued to suffer? It seems inexplicable."

Rogerton conceded, "I've been equally clueless. Despite our persistent queries, the High Cleric never divulged the reasons. We all hoped to hear that we were unique in some way, that he saw in us something no one else could. Maybe he did, but if so, he kept it to himself."

"That's strange," Sven commented. Despite the warmth of the night, an uncanny sensation crawled up his spine. Something about the High Cleric's secretive mission seemed ominous, incongruous.

Yet, he kept his disquiet to himself. Regardless of their unanswered questions, Demetrius affirmed their gratitude, "However, we owe him a lot. Our current existence is thanks to him. So, if he prefers to hold onto his secrets, I believe we should respect that. He has done enough for us to earn that right."

CHAPTER 21: RELIC RUN

A hush enveloped the space around the fire as their storytelling came to an end. The night had woven a curtain of quiet around them, punctuated by the sporadic chirping of nocturnal critters and the soft snap and pop of the campfire. Sven glanced at his two companions, the words spoken between them lingering.

Despite their youthful exuberance and sometimes jarring naivety, he found a certain nobility in their unwavering conviction. Their trust in the High Cleric echoed his own staunch faith in his path as Shatterfist. Although born in diverse circumstances, they were all merely men striving to navigate the complex waters of their destinies.

Their stories bore the scars of hardship, a tale of survival and eventual ascension from the depths of despair, a reflection of their resilient spirits. Sven felt a profound respect welling up within him for these two. He was well-versed in the challenges of life himself, having faced countless trials and tribulations on his journeys. Their shared resolve made them kindred spirits, in a sense.

Upon the conclusion of their heart-wrenching narratives, Sven opted not to regale them with his own tale. "We'll reserve that for another day, lads," he declared, finishing his final morsel of bread and cheese. "Perhaps tomorrow, when we've handed over the relic to the Cleric and we're hoisting mugs of ale in a bustling tavern, that would be a fitting backdrop for my tale."

The two Sons exchanged a glance. "The Cleric frowns upon us gallivanting about in the town," Demetrius disclosed, a note of uncertainty in his voice. "He always reminds us that our tower houses ample ale. It's a rather well-stocked fortress."

Sven chortled, unrolling his bedroll and reclining against it. "Oh, we're certainly heading to the tavern. Your tower, despite its merits, lacks the relaxing ambiance of a local haunt, especially with the Cleric's ever-watchful eyes. A night out would do you both good. Demetrius, you've earned it. As for you, Rogerton—well, only time will tell."

Rogerton's face lit up with excitement at his words. "Does this mean you'll allow me to accompany you? Can I learn to become an adventurer like you?"

Sven let out a resigned sigh, "We'll discuss this later. For now, I seek the comfort of sleep."

He stretched his limbs, sinking into his bedroll, and was fast asleep within moments. When he awoke with the dawn's light, he found Rogerton diligently saddling the horses and readying their gear.

The lad is eager. Sven observed.

Yet, Sven wasn't prepared to entertain any promises just yet. He had his hands full mentoring Demetrius—a single apprentice was perhaps more than enough for now.

Is that how I see him, as an apprentice? He wondered.

Sven shook his head, chiding himself. He had to rid himself of such notions. He was only in this world temporarily, and he knew he couldn't offer them the training they so keenly sought.

As they prepared to depart, Sven took one final glance at the ominous entrance of the Wailing Chambers.

"Farewell, you dreary pit." Sven called out.

And then they were on their way. Sven dictated a brisk pace back to Westville, deliberately allowing minimal time for chatter. Fortunately, they encountered no demonic entities en route. Perhaps news of their victory over the hydra had put the sinister beings on alert. He certainly wished for it to be so.

Upon their arrival at the tower, Sven dismounted his horse swiftly, striding up the steps two at a time, his sack of precious relics in tow. Demetrius struggled to keep pace, while Rogerton attended to the horses and their gear.

Demetrius' eyes widened in surprise. "What's the rush, Sven? Where are you heading?"

"To deliver this relic to the High Cleric. The faster we conclude this business, the sooner we can head to the tavern."

"But the Cleric doesn't appreciate being disturbed," Demetrius protested. "He usually approaches us at his convenience."

He shot back, unfazed, "Well, he'll have to adjust. Since he's keen on sending me on these quests, he can very well accept the spoils on my time and terms."

Sven cast a glance back at the younger men, his expression firm. "You know, in your 'holy texts,' I believe there's mention of me owning and operating one of the greatest taverns across the continents?"

Demetrius nodded without hesitation. "Yes, that's correct. The Adventurer's Rest, isn't it? The chronicles often point out that proficiency in one domain doesn't guarantee mastery in another. It's presented as a sort of cautionary anecdote."

Sven couldn't help but chuckle at the memory, a slightly uncomfortable shuffling accompanying his mirth. "Yes, that sounds about right. If it weren't for Ash and Lloyd, I would have driven that place into oblivion."

He paused, a faraway look in his eyes as the memories unfurled. The loud chatter and laughter of patrons, the smell of roasting meat, and the clinking of ale mugs. The Adventurer's Rest had been a hub of camaraderie and celebration, of sharing tales occasionally embellished but well-meaning tales.

"But, despite everything," Sven continued, his voice growing softer as a somber look crept over his face, "that place was my refuge, my anchor. It was what truly brought me home."

There was a pause, the weight of his words hanging in the chilly evening air. The jovial adventurer they had been accompanying seemed to have been replaced with a reflective figure burdened by shadows of the past. His eyes spoke of tales only he could see, distant as he journeyed back into memories.

"Adventuring isn't as glamourous as the stories make it out to be, not just my stories, any stories," he began, his voice barely above a whisper. "Yes, there's thrill, excitement, a sense of discovery and power, but...there are also losses, great and small. You don't always notice them at first, but they pile up and up until at some point you realize you're just carrying around the things you've survived, and sometimes the things that only you survived."

The two Sons watched him, their eyes wide and attentive. This was a side of Sven they had never seen or known of. He usually wore an easy grin, although stern when the occasion called. They Sven they'd seen had been steady and dependable. But now, they saw a man shaped by both victories and defeats, one who had lived through the complexities of an adventurer's life.

"Friends who stood by your side one moment could be lost in the blink of an eye," Sven continued, his voice barely a whisper. "Friends, enemies, everyone in between reduced to memories in the cruel, unforgiving wilderness. You carry on, not because you want to, but because you have to."

His gaze focused inward and he stopped for a second before continuing.

"And when you finally make it back, weary and battered, sometimes there's no familiar comfort to welcome you. Home doesn't exist for you. I...I returned only to find the home I grew up in was no more and Ma Riley...she was gone."

Sven's stories were often filled with exciting exploits and light-hearted humor. Yet, this time the boys seemed to hold onto his words with solemn looks, as Sven grew poignant in the telling. In their wide eyes and hushed silence, Sven saw the Sons processing this new information. It wasn't just about teaching them the ropes of adventuring, but also preparing them for the realities they might face.

"When I came home." Sven continued, "Finally came home. Nobody knew me, not really. I had been gone so long that whatever place might have been left for me had been passed on to another. I was luckier than most. I had one person who stuck with me through those days, and that's a lot more than most people get."

"You see, you may not have ever heard of this, but there was a time when this world was threatened by a plague of undeath." Sven explained, "If you've never seen what that looks like, let me assure you, it is for the best. There is nothing like coming across an empty town and village only to be beset by ghouls and zombies on the roads. I am saving you many of the details. But in those dark days, it was a bitter job, and somebody had to do it."

Sven continued, a bitter smile on his weathered face, "Recognition isn't always the lot of heroes. Guild affiliated heroes don't put themselves into danger for the sake of glory, but to safeguard life, keep the peace, or return to it. Our fight against the plague wasn't about carving out a legend for ourselves, but about sheltering our world and saving those who we could."

Demetrius, ever steadfast in his convictions, seemed taken aback by this newfound depth in Sven. He said, "Yet, Sven, the deeds of heroes are deserving of honor. They serve as beacons of hope, and examples for all of us to look up to."

Sven responded, the wisdom of years apparent in his voice, "And what about those heroes that get forgotten? The silent warriors who fight the good fight without expecting applause?"

In that moment, Sven wasn't just a legend to the Sons, but a battle-hardened veteran carrying the burdens of his past.

"Many did the same things I did," he added. "Adventurers, Rankers, individuals whose deeds have gone unnoticed, their stories untold. They've battled the same monsters, braved the same dangers, shared in the same victories...and suffered the same losses."

Sven's gaze clouded over, his voice almost a whisper, "For a lot of those brave souls, I'm the only one who'll ever recall their names. That's the reality of being an adventurer."

Demetrius looked at Sven, he could tell his words were sinking in. Although he could have done without the reverence that shone there too. "This... this is the wisdom of the one true Sven."

Sven, thinking back on the insights he'd gained over his long life, decided to make a point. "Tell me," he began, his voice steady, "apart from me, who are the other heroes that come to your mind?"

Demetrius and Rogerton exchanged sheepish glances, caught off guard by the question. After a few moments of awkward silence, they both hesitantly mentioned a few names they could remember.

"Well, there's Galen...You saved him from the dungeon?" Rogerton started tentatively.

"And there's Lloyd...the half-elf who works as a bartender," Demetrius added, sounding unsure of himself.

Sven's point hit home. "Let's leave it at that. We need to drop this relic off anyways."

There was an unspoken agreement between the three as they moved on, their steps echoing through the vacant halls of the tower. Demetrius, despite his visible discomfort, followed Sven as they ascended the stone staircase. When they arrived at the ancient door of the tower's sage, Sven rapped thrice, each knock reverberating ominously.

A faint rustling of movement echoed from within, growing louder until the door creaked open reluctantly.

"What do you want?" The grumpy old Cleric

questioned, annoyance seeping into his tone.

"We have something for you," Sven replied with a casualness that seemed to contrast the gravity of their quest. He rummaged through his bag, finally retrieving the radiant orb they'd worked so hard to obtain. He handed it to the Cleric, who squinted at it through his watery eyes, analyzing it with careful scrutiny.

"Well, I suppose this will do," the Cleric conceded, his voice carrying a begrudging acknowledgment.

Sven feigned surprise, "Just 'this will do'? No thank you?"

The old man didn't even blink, "I expect you to be prepared for the next task tomorrow. Rest here for tonight. Our next target is another relic, hidden deep within the Ghost Forest. We need it to conquer the demon."

Sven was unfazed by the old man's gruff demeanor; he had seen worse in his adventures. But young Demetrius looked like he had seen a ghost. "But...we just returned from a quest..."

The old man cut him off with a swift gesture, "Your job is to follow orders, boy. This is why the Sons exist. We've been preparing for this moment."

Demetrius stuttered, struggling to form a

coherent response. Meanwhile, Sven picked up his satchel again, "Alright, let's regroup at the tavern. Demetrius, are you joining?"

The Cleric growled, "We don't need to..."

Ignoring the old man, Sven responded, "Great, see you later!" and quickly descended the stairs. Demetrius followed after a moment, and they collected Rogerton at the tower's entrance.

"We're headed to the Blind Goat," Sven stated as he set a brisk pace. "I was there earlier, just before the demon attack. Decent enough place."

"But the Cleric will be furious," Demetrius interjected, huffing and puffing as he tried to match Sven's stride. "He hates being disobeyed."

"Don't worry about him. I've dealt with worse," Sven said, although he hadn't quite encountered an organization as strange as the Sons of Sven. But he kept this detail to himself.

CHAPTER 22: TAVERN

The Blind Goat wasn't just any old watering hole, it was the kind of joint where both saints and sinners could find a bit of solace. The creaky wooden door, groaning under the burden of countless stories, stood as a silent invitation. As they stepped through, they were welcomed into a world that was as rugged as it was warm.

The room was filled with a collection of individuals as diverse as they come. Off to one side, a gaggle of grizzled old mercenaries roared with laughter, their glasses clinking in a boisterous salute. Across the room, a secretive pair sat huddled in their own little bubble, their whispers adding to the room's symphony of hushed tones and murmurs.

Regulars were scattered around the place, their faces as much a part of the tavern as the worn wooden stools. The norm in here was to nod, grunt a quick greeting and return to your own business—it was a place that thrived on anonymity and unspoken stories.

Then there was Matthew, the heart and soul of this shady operation. A stocky man with a gleaming dome for a head and a permanent shadow gracing his cheeks. He leaned against the bar with the air of someone who'd seen it all. His eyes lit up when he saw Sven, breaking his facade of well-rehearsed indifference.

"Oi! If it ain't good ol' Tom!" Matthew's voice boomed, bouncing off the walls, "Pull up a stool, lads. First round's on the house!"

With a nonchalant wave, Sven led his companions towards the welcoming refuge of the bar. As they made themselves comfortable, the distinct ambiance of the Blind Goat seeped into their senses—the gentle hum of idle chatter, the clinking of glasses, the spontaneous eruption of raucous laughter.

This place was a sanctuary in its own right, a brief escape from a world teetering on the edge. For Sven, a seasoned warrior who had braved the roughest terrains, this lively, somewhat seedy environment felt just right. He thought to himself, looking around with a smirk, "This...this is my kind of *fun*."

Demetrius and Rogerton, looked around warily, taking in the rough-hewn surroundings with wide-eyed apprehension.

"Are you sure about this place, Sven?" Demetrius asked, his voice barely above a whisper as he cast a sidelong glance at a boisterous group of mercenaries nearby.

Without turning, Sven picked up his mug, the cold condensation trickling down his hand. He took a long, slow gulp of his ale, feeling the frothy liquid slide down his throat and warm his belly. Lowering the mug from his lips, he wiped the remnants of the brew off his growing beard and turned to face the younger men, a mischievous glint in his eyes.

"Not even a little," he responded with a lopsided grin, "But the beer's about right." He raised his mug in a mock salute and took another hearty swig. "Also, why we're here, I would like you two to call me by my real name. Tom." The two boys nodded.

"Oi, you're still in one piece then?" Matthew

drawled, slapping the wooden counter. "Didn't reckon the demons got to you yet."

"Just about," Sven replied, waving dismissively. "A round of dark ale, Matthew. One for each of us."

He glanced back at Demetrius and Rogerton. Their eyes darted nervously around the bustling tavern, like cornered rabbits in a den of foxes. It dawned on him—was this their first time in a place like this?

Seeing their silence as consent, he said, "Make it two more ales."

Securing a secluded corner table, he ushered the young ones over while Matthew busied himself with their drinks. The lads tried to look casual, but their stiff posture betrayed their unease. The arrival of frothy ales seemed to loosen them a bit as they took tentative sips.

"Food, Matthew," Sven said, leaning back into his chair. The last two nights of travel and cold grub had ignited a hunger in him. "Got anything filling?"

"Reckon three of those new hamburgers I've been perfecting?" Matthew proposed, his eyes lighting up at the prospect. "And a heap of fries?"

Demetrius and Rogerton exchanged puzzled

looks. The Cleric had spoken a little about Earth when the Son's sang their epic about him. To them this sounded like food from Sven's world. Sven seeing their recognition, shrugged and nodded. "Sounds about right. Fire away, Matthew."

Matthew bustled off to work his magic, leaving them to enjoy their drinks amidst the rowdy din of the tavern.

"Not half bad," Demetrius conceded, a hint of surprise in his voice. "Actually kind of relaxing."

"Better than the stuffy tower?" Sven prodded, a smirk playing on his lips.

"Worlds better," Demetrius affirmed.

Rogerton, who'd been silent till then, turned to Sven. "You promised a tale when we hit a tavern. We've got our ale, and here we are. Time to deliver, Sven…er, Tom."

Sven heaved a sigh, glancing at the expectant faces. He could buy time, stall till their food arrived or their second round was poured. But he'd asked them to be patient, and they had been. Maybe it was time for that tale.

He mused on what narrative to weave. His past was a minefield of memories, some of them gleaming with valor and companionship, others tarnished with betrayal and loss. There was a multitude of tales at his disposal—from old comrades to darker times—but few he wanted to share with the young Sons.

"No, not the old days with Basequin, Rabbit, and Galen," he muttered under his breath. *No tales of treachery or my fall. That's too dark, too painful.* He thought. He didn't wish to revisit the story of his fatal betrayal and subsequent rebirth as a demon-corpse through Ash's sorcery, not on this light-hearted occasion. His departure from the Kingdom of White Lions was a dull and familiar story too, one that the lads probably had already heard in bits and pieces.

He finally settled on a narrative, a tale from a less complicated time. Clearing his throat, he began, "I suppose I could tell you about an unusual acquaintance of mine—a hydra."

Both boys perked up, their previous discomfort fading into the background. This was what they had been waiting for—a tale from their seasoned companion, a peek into a world of adventure that they were just beginning to experience.

Sven grinned at their reaction. "Yes, a hydra. An enemy at first, then a begrudging co-worker, and finally...well, as close to a friend as a hydra can get."

A ripple of surprise passed through the young adventurers. "A hydra?" Demetrius echoed, his eyes widening. "You befriended a hydra? But...how?"

Sven chuckled, leaning back in his chair. "It was a during my latter years, I used to guide adventurers not much older than you lads," he said. "It was in the Dungeon of the Woods and the Northern Forests. Occasionally I'd accompany lower ranking adventurers through the dungeon and help them defeat the boss. One such boss was an elemental hydra."

He paused, savoring a mouthful of the dark ale. The mention of the hydra brought back a flood of memories. This creature wasn't like the malevolent beast they'd faced recently. This hydra had been...different. It had been a stickler for rules and liked protocol.

Sven searched for the right words. This hydra had been gruff, often exasperated by the folly of inexperienced adventurers. Yet, beneath the coarse exterior was a strange sense of loyalty. He recalled how the hydra had sacrificed itself in a battle against a demon. *Had it ever regenerated, or was its death permanent?* The uncertainty lingered, unanswered.

"He was an agreeable creature," he finally said, his tone reflecting mild nostalgia. "We had a unique arrangement. I'd get him a crate of honey mead, and in return, he'd give me a summoning token. He even lent a claw in defending Adventurer's Rest a couple of times. It wasn't a bad gig for either of us."

Demetrius' puzzlement was clear. "Nice? Friends? Mutually beneficial?" He frowned, scratching his head. "But he was a dungeon boss. Weren't you supposed to—"

Sven intercepted his question with a knowing smile. "Fight him? Kill him? Yes, and yes. But he was a dungeon boss. Surely, you two understand. In the golden era of dungeoneering, creatures within those mystical confines would respawn. Powerful warriors like myself had ample opportunity to explore interactions far beyond the usual slash and hack routine. To put it simply, I was leagues ahead of the hydra in strength and it had grown tired of me killing it regularly. So it began talking to me."

This notion stood in stark contrast to the reality of their current world. Unlike the cyclical life-and-death dance within the dungeon, existence was an irreversible linear march. Death was final.

The conversation came to a pause as Matthew emerged from the kitchen, arms laden with plates of substantial burgers. He carefully set them down on their table, the dishes clattering gently. With a brief retreat back to the kitchen, he returned with a large bowl of golden, crisp fries.

"Enjoy your meal, lads," he offered, a tinge of anxiety lining his voice. "I trust it meets your expectations."

The silence that stretched through the tavern was palpable. All the patrons were absorbed by the tale spun by Sven, their good time stilled by the lackluster ending.

"Hah," finally, an aged regular broke the stillness, his laughter lined with teasing. "Quite the *melancholic* tale that, Sven. I was expecting great battles, swooning maidens and amazing relics!"

A ripple of laughter spread across the room, lifting the mood, especially when Sven's hearty laughter joined them. Seizing the moment of joviality, Sven dug into his burger. The taste exploded in his mouth—perfectly cooked patty, the juiciness of the meat mingling with the toasted crunch of the roll. Matthew, he thought, could have made a living as a fine chef back on Earth.

"Suppose it was a bit of a downer," Sven conceded, wiping a bit of sauce from the corner of his mouth. "Apologies for the lack of grand battles and heroic feats. I'll delve into my memory and come up with something more thrilling for next time."

Demetrius was quick to reassure him. "It's fine...Tom! We've heard countless tales of your heroics and bravery from when we were kids. I reckon we still remember a good many of them."

Excitement gleamed in Rogerton's eyes, eager to contribute. "How about we share one of those stories?"

But Sven held up a hand, deferring his offer. "Another time, perhaps. For now, let's simply revel in the comfort of our meal."

Leaning back in his chair, he scanned the tavern. The residents were lively, their spirits undampened despite the looming threats they faced. A stark contrast to the eerie unease that the Sons' tower held. *Good folks,* Sven mused, *they truly are.*

A thought then began to surface in his mind,

one that he had often found himself suppressing. He was needed here, in this world threatened by danger. The bindings that tied him as a summoned hero would not last forever, and he was once again in his prime. A world where he was respected, admired, and powerful.

And yet, a tug in his heart reminded him of his other life, the one he had left behind. The life where his beloved wife, Ash, and their daughter Kaleigh, were waiting. The familiar warmth of home, the soft laughter of his little girl, the shared moments with Ash—a life that was equally compelling.

His gaze softened as he looked around the tavern, filled with laughter and camaraderie. What if he stayed here, he wondered, not as a temporary savior, but as a permanent resident? The thought was tempting, but also terrifying. And for now, it was merely a thought.

AFTERWORD

Thank you for your time and giving this book a chance. For further interaction with fellow readers and authors, consider joining our online communities.

1. The Hunter's Den on Discord: https://discord.gg/htzB3CW62S
2. LitRPG Books on Facebook: https://www.facebook.com/groups/LitRPG.books
3. LitRPG Society on Facebook: https://www.facebook.com/groups/LitRPGsociety
4. LitRPG Releases on Facebook: https://www.facebook.com/groups/LitRPGReleases
5. LitRPG subreddit: https://www.reddit.com/r/litrpg/
6. Amazon Book Club: https://www.amazon.com/abc/detail/amzn1.club.bookclub.7aba3a46-af44-70be-7bf8-5f91cf522ead?ref_=abc_aa_bdp_r_ds_imw_ibc